THE NIP AND TUCK WAR

by

Mary Mian

Illustrated by Beth and Joe Krush

This story, like other fairy stories, has a King and a Princess, but it is really about a goatherd who got animals to come to the aid of man. When the wicked Baron Gnarl locked up the King and the Princess of Croon, Nip (with the ability to talk to *all* animals and birds) knew he had to go to war with whatever army he could get together. The two-legged animals didn't like the four-legged ones, and the birds and hornets were in a separate class, so there was a lot of bickering. It was hilarious — the horses in a jousting tournament suddenly became bucking broncos, spilling their riders; the whole court itched every night from mosquito bites, and humans couldn't trust a pigeon or a dog to behave as expected any more. Nip and his animal friends won the war and a Princess, too. Then the animals went back to doing whatever they did best.

* * * *·

Classification and Dewey Decimal: Fiction (Fic)

About the Author:

When Mary Shipman married Aristide Mian, a French sculptor, they divided their time between Paris and Santa Fe, New Mexico. This produced a strange mixture of interests, language and costumes — French silk scarves and cowboy boots. Mrs. Mian, whose stories have appeared in the *New Yorker*, found herself writing for children when she acquired a grandchild.

About the Illustrators:

BETH AND JOE KRUSH met at the Philadelphia Museum School of Art where they were both studying. They now live near Valley Forge with their son.

The
Nip *and* Tuck
War

MARY MIAN

Illustrated by Beth and Joe Krush

1967 FIRST CADMUS EDITION
THIS SPECIAL EDITION IS PUBLISHED BY ARRANGEMENT WITH
THE PUBLISHERS OF THE REGULAR EDITION
HOUGHTON MIFFLIN COMPANY

BY

E. M. HALE AND COMPANY
EAU CLAIRE, WISCONSIN

In the country of Croon, during the reign of Boldo the Ninth, a short war took place known as the War of the Glorious Rescue. So the historian calls it, but in a footnote he adds that the people of Croon called it the Nip and Tuck War. He gives no reason why, and very few facts about the war itself. Maybe he didn't know them. Maybe he thought no one would believe him.

There was a reason, of course. For the same reason, wars Napoleon fought in were called Napoleonic wars. Everybody knew Napoleon was in them. Everybody knew Nip and Tuck were in this one. If they hadn't been, then no war. Though, as time passed, the Croonians came to be a bit hazy about it, and wouldn't always give the same reason. When the children asked the old men, "Why was it called the Nip and Tuck War, Grandpa?" one would say, "Well, it was the horses . . ."

"No no! it was the hornets . . ."

The beginning, you might say, was a summer day when King Boldo the Ninth went hunting in Greengrim Forest. We can still see Boldo in his statue on horseback in the public square of Barracoon, one and only city of Croon. At least, the head is believed to be that of Boldo the Ninth, since that one is missing from the interchangeable set made to fit the statue, now in the State Museum. It shows him as a cheerful, bouncy sort of king, with a curly beard. The body appears to be waving its troops on to war, and probably was, since it was made for Boldo the First, but Boldo the Ninth had never done so. He was more likely to be shouting "Tally-ho!" And the Croonians were more likely to be at home, sleeping off a lunch that was more like a Sunday dinner.

Today, Croon is, of course, a progressive republic, governed by a President, a Congress, an Income Tax Bureau, the Unions and the P.T.A., like the rest of us. But in those far-off days the King ruled, if he cared to. Boldo didn't. All he cared about was hunting.

He wasn't even a good hunter, being very nearsighted, which he wouldn't admit, even to himself. When he shot at a pheasant, it flew away, or it turned out to be a stray hen. The deer, he said, ran faster than they used to. People stayed away from the woods when he was there. His hunters covered up for him; they pretended it was his shot that hit the mark, and he didn't look too closely, I'm afraid. Even a well-meaning king can be spoiled by the kind of treatment he gets.

The animals were pretty tired of it. The country was going to the dogs and the hunters, they said. Try to raise a family, with that to contend with! Some of them had already moved out, and a lot more were thinking about it.

Even Boldo, who was not a bad sort really, though none too bright, was beginning to find things rather boring. "Ah, for the old days!" he used to sigh. "Quests after dragons and fabulous monsters, you know! Quests that lasted for months, for years! *That* was a hunt!" But no fabulous monsters had been seen in the kingdom

2

within the memory of anyone he knew.

His wife, Queen Florina, had died when their child, Princess Cristella, was very young and this had been a heavy grief to Boldo. When she was alive, he had taken an interest in his kingdom because she did, and so had the people of Croon. She loved them and they her, and, with her encouragement, they made Croon a model kingdom, for the times. Once she was gone, Boldo had lost heart, and the people had gone back to their lazy ways. The rule was left to the King's advisers, who were quite satisfied with this arrangement. Chief among them were the Lord Chancellor, Baron Gnarl of Castle Lumbago, and the King's elderly aunt, the Countess of Bile, known as Dame Migraine, who between them ran things pretty much to suit themselves. The others were a so-so lot, and thought only of filling their own pockets. In a democracy, of course, we wouldn't put up with that sort of thing for a minute.

Gnarl was one minister who wasn't satisfied.

"Here I am, a man of my keen wits, a mere baron!" he used to say to his wife, Rubeola. "And here are you, my dear, with your queenly beauty, a mere baroness. And our son, Cramp, a mere baron's son. And there he is — that lout of a king, only out of the saddle to sleep. And no queen at all, so very few parties for you to outshine the other women. And our handsome son . . . Hmmmm! A marriage made in heaven, you'd say, but heaven often needs a helping hand!"

Unfortunately for Gnarl's plans, Princess Cristella didn't like Cramp at all. After she'd seen him at her birthday party, pulling wings off butterflies and throwing a

3

nest of baby birds in the river, she wouldn't have him at another party. But Rubeola, who thought a crown would set off her other curves, listened to her husband's grumbling. We can guess at the turn their discussions took by what came out of them.

One afternoon, when the King had fidgeted through a council, Gnarl had shown himself most helpful. "No need for Your Majesty to stay — I'll take care of everything!"

The King bounded from the room, and Gnarl followed him. "Just a word, Your Majesty — if you're hunting in Greengrim Forest, near my land, stay away from that old quarry. A strange beast around there lately, my people tell me. Sheep been disappearing by the dozen. One man came in with a fantastic tale. Fire-breathing dragon — claimed to have seen it. Nonsense, of course. But *something's* eating those sheep, and Your Majesty had best stay out of danger."

"Danger?" said the King, pricking up his ears. "Fire-breathing . . . ?"

"Grass burnt black," admitted Gnarl. "Strange foot prints, too — big claws . . . But Your Majesty mustn't go near there. I'll clear the beast out."

"Gnarl," said the King, "I'll look into this. I've been waiting for it."

"But, Your Majesty . . ."

"Not another word!"

And so the hunt next morning went deep into Greengrim Forest. Early on, the King managed to slip away from the others. He hadn't told them of Gnarl's warning, so they were not alarmed at his disappearing; he had done it before. It would not be easy for him to get lost. Croon was a very small country shaped like a sausage, lying between two mountain ranges, the Calomels and the Gorge Rising. At one end the Liverish River plunged down the cliffs, and then, as though the valley had put it to sleep, meandered along to a deep gorge at the other end, and out. Protected by these mountains, Croon had

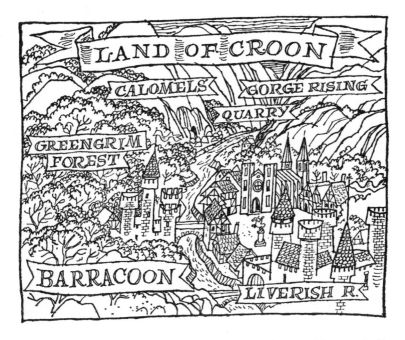

forgotten what it was like to have enemies, and least of all were its people awake to enemies within their own borders.

Greengrim Forest was little visited by the comfortable Croonians — that was what they liked to call themselves. Wolves, bears and wild boars lived there, and only Boldo and his huntsmen went far into it. Today Boldo made straight for the old quarry, and came at last to the rocky face of a cliff in the side of the hill where the stone had been quarried, leaving gashes and holes.

His horse stopped, sniffed, and whinnied. In front of one cave the grass was badly scorched, strewn with bones. Not bleached bones — bloody, as though recently gnawed.

Boldo dismounted, tied his frightened horse to a tree, and approached the cave. He was not lacking in courage, though he was in good sense. At the cave mouth he stopped and listened. He heard a rattle, mixed with a whistle that rose and fell. Could it be snoring?

Boldo drew a long hunting knife and went inside.

The passage was high enough for him to stand upright, but it turned to one side, and grew dim and shadowy. The snoring grew louder. The passage opened into a large cave. Boldo's shortsighted eyes could just make out a dark shape coiled at the farther end. Two red eyes opened, and the rattling stopped.

Boldo knew then how foolish he had been. He stepped back, his sword at the ready.

"Hail, O King!" said a raspy voice.

Boldo peered at the beast, and saw, in the half-light, a huge and hideous head, all greenish scales and grinning teeth, and, at each side, claws like sickles.

"Hail, O . . . who, um, do I have the pleasure . . . ?" he said.

"Gulp, the Dragon," said the voice. "Full fain was I to behold thee."

"Full — what?" was all Boldo could say.

"Glad, you fool!" snapped the dragon. "Hast thou not wit to wot the elder speech?"

6

"Oh, we don't speak that way nowadays, you know, except for jousts and that sort of thing," Boldo said. "Haven't for over a century."

"Well, dragons do! What's a century to a dragon?"

"How do you know me?"

"Scouting around by night, forsooth," said the dragon. "I have wings." They clanked on the floor behind him.

"Where do you come from? They all said there were no more dragons in any civilized country."

"From an uncivilized country up north," said the dragon. His grin was like a crocodile's grin, but worse. It smoked.

"How do you like it here?" said Boldo politely. He hadn't expected a dragon to talk.

"Full well," said the dragon. "Except for the food. A dragon, sirrah, hath but a queasy stomach. Sheep suit it not. Wit thou well, I don't wike wool. Hrrrmp! I mean, wool it liketh me not."

"I'll send you picnic baskets," said the King hastily. "My Chief Chef, Cherijello, is excellent. Barbecued lamb — lamb stew — no wool!"

The smoke puffed up faster. "Methinks, sire, you have a daughter."

"No no!" said the King. "Only an aunt. A great-aunt."

"No good, Boldy!" said the dragon. "I saw her with these eyes, eftsoons — ekewhiles — last night, to be exact. A comely maid! I want to meet her. Have her here by six tomorrow night, or 'ware! I shall take umbrage!"

"Who's he?" said Boldo distractedly. "No one by that name in the castle, that I know of." . .

"Idiot!" yelled the dragon. "I shall lose my temper,

7

that means. And you know what *that* means, Boldy, old boy! Scorched earth!" Smoke poured out now in such a cloud that Boldo coughed and choked, and a small flame shot up. "Thy people in jeopardy! Those that escape me homeless, their crops and stores, ashes. A wasteland, fell and dismal! Think of that!"

"I'll — I'll think about it." He would send the whole army, or they would trick the dragon . . .

"And hearken, Boldy! Think not to cozen me by sending the daughter of the Chief Chef in her stead! I wot that wile!"

"You wot that what?" said poor Boldo, quite confused.

"I know that trick!" bellowed the dragon. "Have her here, or, by my grumbling guts and gizzard, thou'll see what I can do! And think not to smoke me out — I have another exit. Play the caitiff and thou'lt rue the day!"

"My daughter is — rather small," pleaded the King. "If I make you such a feast as has never been seen, that will last a month . . ."

"If she's not here tomorrow — " snarled the dragon — "but I wot she will be!"

"I wot she won't!" shouted Boldo. "I defy you!" He gathered all his strength, and threw his sword at the dragon. When it hit, smoke and sparks rushed up; but the knife fell.

"Witless wight! A wart thou wert!" snickered the dragon. "I'd shrivel thee like a moth, but I want the princess! Now go, before I huff up a forest fire! Away with thee! Hence!"

Boldo henced.

WHILE Boldo is riding homeward, in a calamitous state of mind, let us take a look at the Princess.

Cristella had been moping, alone in her bedroom, where, her tennis master having sprained his wrist, she had been sent to take a nap. So seldom was Cristella allowed any time to herself that she didn't know what to do with it. Dame Migraine disapproved of the way Boldo spent his time, though she was glad enough for matters to be left in her hands, and she saw to it Cristella had none to waste. "Your Highness, time for your history, or music, or riding, or tennis, or dancing . . ." or, "You're to give the prize at the Harvest Festival — ride in the parade as honorary captain of the Royal Guards." All very grand, but when Cristella saw idle children in the street, doing nothing and having a good time at it, she felt a cold pinch of loneliness.

Small fun it was playing with children of the nobles, carefully chosen by Dame Migraine, because they always let her win — and that horrid Cramp was always there, until she had refused to leave her room if he came, in spite of her great-aunt's anger. What she had seen him do was nothing to what he boasted he could do to any animal that had the bad luck to fall into his hands.

And Cristella did love animals, though Dame Migraine didn't allow her to have pets — they gave trouble, they were dirty, had fleas — why didn't she play with Biscuit?

Biscuit was Dame Migraine's own dog, named when he was a puppy, and before he had swollen into an enormous popover. He was known about the court as Grumble, because of the rumbling noises he gave out, what with overfeeding and bad temper. Cristella tried to be friends with Grumble, but he wanted no friends, only servants. He didn't beg: he commanded. And he preferred those servants who bowed before addressing him.

That day, the maid of honor in Cristella's room had dozed off in her chair. Cristella wasn't sleepy; she tossed about. The box of costumes that had been sent up that morning for her to choose from, for the gypsy dance she was to do at Señora Tippito's recital, was still lying on the floor. Among the lot had been a plain, dark little dress that must have got in by mistake; they hadn't bothered to try it on. The Princess pulled it out of the box, and, for something to do, tried it on.

In the glass, she looked different, unlike herself. Her hair, silver-gilt and smooth, was hidden under a dark kerchief. She wondered what it would be like, to be that girl. If she were, no one would fuss over her, tell her what to do. She would do what she pleased.

"If I were outside, in this dress, I don't believe they would know me. I'd like to try . . . why not? Everyone's asleep . . . I *will* try!"

She had overheard the maids of honor whispering about ·a gate in the castle wall they used at night, leaving the key hidden in the mouth of a stone lion close by. Why not use it herself? She crept by the maid and stole out.

No one in sight; the footman had gone to chat with a

friend. Down a back stairway now, and past a few lackeys, half asleep, who glanced at her indifferently — they didn't know her! They took her for some kitchen maid! She felt wings on her shoulders that carried her out into the court and down to the wall.

There, the lion's head — and there, the key, right in the mouth! She tried it in the gate, and the gate opened.

Now, the key in that hole in the apple tree! She ran along the path, through the orchard, and saw another path that led up over the fields, into the hills beyond.

One or two people went by, but they hardly looked at her. It gave her the funniest feeling. "I'm invisible!" she said. "I can go where I like!" She ran on and up.

She could look down now at her own castle; she had never been able to do that before, and it was more beautiful than she had known. Like most castles in the old days, it had once been surrounded by a moat, but Queen Florina had had it filled in. A nuisance, she said, and bred mosquitoes. What did they need of a moat? They had no enemies. Below her lay the Liverish, shining, and the humped arches of St. Vigoro's bridge that connected the castle with the town of Barracoon. There was a tall watch tower and gate at the castle end of the bridge, rising from the wall which held the castle in a girdle. Outside it were the lists, where tourneys were held, and parks, and pleasure walks, storehouses and stables; inside was the circle of towers that formed the castle, its bedchambers, halls and audience rooms, its dining halls, pantries and kitchens. All her life was there below her, and, for the first time, she could stand off and look at it.

She turned her back, and hurried up to the hilly country behind. No more tilled fields — rough pastures. She came to a hedge, and behind it she heard music. Pipes and bells. She followed the path, through a hole in the hedge, and found herself at the edge of a rocky meadow. Crickets were singing, butterflies flitting. Goats were gamboling, nibbling at the hedge — all sizes and colors of goats, each with a bell tied to its neck. Their horns curled about like shells. On a rock was their herd, playing his pipes — a boy of near her own age, roughly dressed. As she stood there, he began to sing, and the song wasn't like any she had ever heard.

> *Come, all you goats who are plowing and sowing!*
> *Call up your friends, for it's time to be going.*
> *Cows who are sitting on eggs, let them be now —*
> *Hens cleaning house, come along, you are free now!*
>
> > *Didn't you hear? it's a holiday today!*
> > *Dance with me, dance with me, olee-olay!*
> > *Which of you all will be Queen of the May?*
>
> *Fish, no more building your nests in the trees,*
> *Quit singing lullabies, dogs, to your fleas.*
> *Cats in the kitchen, stop cooking your dinners —*
> *Frogs in the pulpit, stop preaching to sinners!*
>
> > *Didn't you hear? etc. . . .*
>
> *Leave off your washing, old mother raccoon!*
> *Foxes, stop feeding baby birds with a spoon —*
> *Shut your books, rabbits, and lay them aside now —*
> *Hop on my back, and we'll all take a ride now!*
>
> > *Didn't you hear? etc. . . .*

She must have moved, because he turned and saw her.

He had sharp eyes, a mop of black hair, and a big smiling mouth that didn't look respectful.

She walked up to him. She was so used to people rising and bowing to her that she was surprised when he only looked up and said "Hi!" But she remembered she wasn't a princess now, and said "Hi!" too.

"You're no gypsy!" said the boy, looking at her. "You're too clean."

She didn't know what to say. He pulled a coin out of his pocket and held it out to her. She drew back.

"You're no gypsy!" he said. "Gypsies tell fortunes for money."

He took his pipes and played a curlicue of an air on it. "You're no gypsy," he said. "Gypsies dance."

"Well, I can do that," she said, and she danced the gypsy dance she had learned that morning. At the end she sank to her knees and looked to him for the applause she was used to. But he only said, "That's a skip-hopper."

"A what?"

"A dance that's only steps you have learned. One-two, one-two-three! A real dance is a sky-hopper. Like fire dancing in the wind, because it can't help it."

She was furious. "I learned that dance from Señora Tippito, the very best teacher!"

"Real dances aren't learned," he said. "They're already in you."

"You're just an ignorant, dirty boy!"

"I like it that way," he said lazily.

"You're just like one of your goats!"

"They have fun," he said. "Do you? You don't look it."

13

She turned to leave, a princess again. One of the goats pranced up and butted her in the stomach and knocked her down. She waited for the boy to pick her up, but he only laughed, so, for the first time, she picked herself up. She wanted to cry, but she knew he would only laugh the harder.

He was not looking at her now, but at two men in the next field, coming down the path. She thought of telling them he had been rude to her; then he would be punished.

"There's two of your people," he said. "If you're a gypsy. But you're not, are you?"

Then he did something strange; he pulled her down to the grass, scooped up a handful of dust from the path and rubbed it all over her face and arms. "Too clean!" he said. She scrambled to her feet, unable to say a word. "Don't talk! And look stupid! That should be easy!"

The two men came up to them, and stared at Cristella. She had never seen such men; they looked rough and sly. "Gitana?" said one of them, and laughed. "Where you find her?"

"I blew her out of my pipes," said the boy.

"Then blow another," said the man. "We take this one."

"No," said the boy. "She's my sister."

"Your father hate to lose her? Pay money for her?"

"He wouldn't pay a penny — he hasn't got any. He's the herd."

"Nice girl," said the man. "You come away with us?"

Cristella began to tremble, but she said nothing.

"Can't she come?" said the man to the boy. He took

14

out a silver coin and twiddled it.

The boy scratched his head, and Cristella's blood froze when he said, as though it were a matter of little importance, "Sure!"

The gypsy took hold of Cristella's arm. "We treat her good," he said.

"Sure," said the boy. Then he said, "I'll come too. They don't like us at home. They beat us. They'll be glad to be rid of us."

"Why?" said the gypsy suspiciously.

"Oh, you know," said the boy. "They say we don't work, all we do is eat. With you we won't have to work."

"So?" said the gypsy coldly. "We fix that."

"And my sister has a funny way, they can't stop her," said the boy laughing. "She plays with fire. She burned down our shed, hay and all. She doesn't even know she does it. She's not quite right in the head, and she's dumb — can't talk. She's going to love it at your camp."

The gypsy took his hand off Cristella's arm, and looked doubtful.

"And another funny way she's got," said the boy proudly. "She sleeps with snakes."

"She does?" said both gypsies, staring at Cristella. "Why?"

"Crazy for them," said the boy. "See here!" He thrust his hand into her full sleeve, and pulled out a striped snake. Cristella was startled, but she was more afraid of the gypsies than of the snake.

"Hey, that's a bad one!" The gypsies had jumped back. "Why don't it bite her?"

"It doesn't bite us because it knows us," the boy said.

15

"Snakes like her. That's because she's not quite right."

They stared at Cristella, backing away. She gave a silly giggle, and touched first the snake, and then the man.

"She says you can have it," said the boy. "She always gives snakes to people she likes." He went toward the gypsies, holding out the snake.

The two men turned and hurried off down the path as if a pack of snakes were after them.

The boy waited till they were out of sight, and then he dropped the snake in the grass, where it slid away, and sat down and laughed.

"I was good!" he said. "You weren't bad, either!" he added generously.

"Where did the snake come from?" she asked.

"Under my belt, of course," he said. "They like to roll up and sleep there — keep warm. It's not a bad snake but they didn't know that."

"Snakes do like you, then!"

"Yes," he said briefly. "And other animals. You'd better get home now. You came from the castle, didn't you? You'll be safer there than running around by yourself."

She hesitated. "It's nice here," she said. He scowled. "I'll take you," he said. "You'd likely fall and sprain your ankle or something, you're so silly. Come on." He wheeled her about, and they started off down the hill. But first he spoke to the goats; they appeared to listen, and one of them, a big brown goat with wide horns, long beard and yellow eyes, bleated. "That's Tuck," said the boy. "He's the leader."

Cristella was still offended and angry, but she felt an excitement she had never felt before. He didn't know who she was, he thought she was silly, but she had played up. She hadn't been so bad — he'd said so. She ran ahead of him, eager to show him that she wouldn't sprain her ankle.

Down by the wall, they saw guards hunting about frantically. She had been missed. I won't show them the key, or tell them how I got out, she thought.

The guards caught sight of her, and came up threateningly. Cristella pulled off her kerchief, and her silver-gilt hair fell loose over her shoulders. "That's the Princess!" shouted the guards. Two of them grabbed the boy.

Now he'll be impressed, thought Cristella, and she said, like a princess, "Leave him alone!"

17

The guards looked doubtful. She stamped her foot. "Take your hands off him, I say! I was lost, and he saved me from some very bad men!"

The guards obeyed. The boy was looking at her, but whether he was impressed or not, she couldn't tell. Finally, "You have pretty hair," he said.

"Mind your manners!" shouted the guards. "On your knees! That's no way to address the Princess Cristella!"

He went down on one knee, but he still did not look respectful.

She remembered her own manners. "Won't you come in and let my father thank you? You saved me from those gypsies."

"Thanks," he said, "but I'd best be going back. I left my goats all alone, and you can't do that to goats. There's a saying, when they aren't playing tricks, they're thinking them up."

He stood up, bowed, grinned at her, and turned to leave.

"Wait!" she cried. "Will you come back and see me?"

"I might," he said, grinning, and started off.

"Impudence!" growled the guards.

"Wait!" she cried again. "What's your name?"

"Nip, everyone calls me," he said, and this time he ran out of sight.

3

Few people had heard the goat boy called by any other name but Nip, and nobody knew where he came from.

He had been brought up by the monks of St. Vigoro, the patron of Barracoon, and all they could tell was that, twelve or so years ago, a tall, dark-skinned man, a Moor, they thought, old and gray, but straight, with ragged clothes and a staff, had come to the monastery with a boy of about four. A few rags were knotted about the boy, but it became clear that he wasn't used to wearing anything at all. Though fair-skinned, he was brown all over from the sun, scarred and very dirty, but quite healthy. The old man was dumb but not deaf; he showed them that his tongue had been cut out. The child had not learned to talk, and at times he ran about on all fours like an animal. The old man pointed to him, pointed to the monks, and made it plain that he was leaving the boy in their care. He then put his hand on the boy's head, made him a sort of salaam, and set off down the road. No one had ever seen him again.

The brothers learned later from a few woodchoppers, charcoal-burners and the like that the old man and the boy had been living in a hut, far out in the forest. No one knew where they had come from, or their history. The woodcutters said that, from the old man's ways, they had come from a far land, and he was used to better things.

One of them thought that, since the old man couldn't talk, the boy talked with the animals of the forest, but he was an ignorant man, and the brothers laughed at the idea.

The monks were kind and patient men, if inclined to be fat and lazy like the other Croonians, and the boy learned to wear clothes, to eat at table and not on the floor, to talk, and to wash when he had to. He looked not too different from the other boys they taught, but as to his behavior, they shook their heads. Would he ever be like the others?

Not that he was a bad boy at heart, they said. Cheerful, and willing to do what he was told if he trusted you; if he didn't, nothing could make him. He trusted old Brother Barnabas, who did the cooking; he did not trust Brother Hubertus, who tried to cram reading and writing down his throat. When he was given lines to copy and learn, he threw them in the pond, so the frogs could learn them too, and when the frogs croaked that night at vespers, he laughed, because, he said, they were learning their lines. That earned him a beating.

There was no end to the outrageous stories he told at first, once he decided to talk. When he was sent after a hen that had strayed into the woods, he would come back empty-handed, saying he had met a mother fox and had given her the hen for her hungry children. When he didn't want to water the garden, he would say the birds told him it was going to rain, and it was even more exasperating that it usually did rain. When the portly Abbot rode away on his mare, he went into a fit of laughter, because, he said, the mare was wishing the Abbot had to carry *her*. Another beating, for impudence. He learned to curb his tongue, and keep his comical ideas to himself.

20

Wounded or sick animals he was caring for were all about the place, and he had more pets than could conveniently be kept in a monastery. At one time he had a pet owl, which he trained to walk like the Abbot, and who strutted after the Abbot into chapel one day when there was a visiting high churchman. After that, he was told to get rid of his beasts. But when he was supposed to be doing his lessons, he was usually out of the window and away, off to the woods, where he let all sorts of wild creatures, even wolves, out of traps and snares.

Brother Hubertus had baptized him Salvanippus, which he said was Latin for "Saved from the Jaws." None of the other brothers knew enough Latin to say it wasn't; Brother Hubertus had the reputation of being a Latin scholar, though he seldom opened his books now except to teach a smattering of Church Latin to his boys, and a few songs he must have learned as a boy himself, not at all churchly. The other boys changed the name to Nip, because he did, at first — scratched and bit like a small wild animal. With time, he grew tamer, but the name stuck.

One morning Brother Hubertus sent him to sweep out the chapel. Later he went to see how the work was progressing. He got the surprise of his life.

"The place was full of beasts," he told the others. "Birds flying about and twittering, or perched on the images of the blessed saints! A big rabbit sitting up on his hunkers in front of the altar! Squirrels and mice chasing each other! Salvanippus sweeping the floor . . . I grabbed his broom, I can tell you, and sent them all packing. Last of all, a big toad I hadn't seen went hopping out the door. I cuffed the boy well, but he was up to his ears in impudence — said the chapel was for everybody, so why not for the beasts?"

It was after this the Abbot said he could see what was the matter; Salvanippus had never really stopped thinking of himself as an animal. Since he'd been there, the woods had moved into the monastery. Better put him out

to work in the fields, where he and his beasts could see each other to their heart's content, and where he would not annoy respectable people. The monks were quite willing. Even Brother Barnabas was fed up, what with all the rats and mice about the place, since Nip would let them out of traps. It wasn't a kitchen any more, said Brother Barnabas, it was a rat tavern. And Nip was in his teens now, old enough to be on his own. So they found him work at the castle, herding the goats. Clearly he was too simple-minded for cows, but goats might do. He slept in a shed near the goats, and was given his bread and cheese and a leather flask of wine with the other herds.

Most of his time was spent up in the pasture with the goats, or wandering on the edge of the woods with them, since goats prefer leaves to grass. There were no complaints about his care of them; they all flourished, and he never lost any.

The other herds made fun of him, saying he was half goat, but they brought him their ailing animals to care for, and he usually cured them.

What nobody realized was that Nip could still speak the animals' language. He had been careful not to let people know this; he thought, first, they would not believe him, and, second, if they did, they would burn him as a wizard. Queen Florina had disapproved of burning witches and wizards, but she was gone now, so you couldn't tell. Even if they didn't burn him, they might shut him up in a dungeon, and that would be worse. At best, they would treat him like a freak, and make him show off his powers. So he kept his own counsel.

And so, when Princess Cristella had offered to take him in the castle to be thanked by her father, he had refused. Walls of any kind he mistrusted, and the King's castle had the thickest walls around. He hadn't done anything much; it had been fun. Better not put his foot in what might turn out to be a trap.

True, the King might have given him a gold piece, but

it would have cost him more in the end. He shrugged, and went on back to his goats.

As he played his pipes, he thought how pretty was that long silver hair. How it would sweep about, if she could *really* dance! He believed he could teach her. He had taught his goats to dance, and he saw no reason why princesses should be harder to teach than goats.

4

Bоldo, back from his meeting with the dragon, and Cristella, back from her meeting with Nip, were dining alone with Dame Migraine. Alone except for Grumble, who lay by his mistress' chair, accepting the choicer bits of chicken.

It was a silent meal, and Dame Migraine remarked several times that His Majesty had no appetite and looked as though he were coming down with something. Chills, caught out hunting, she said, had often proved fatal, as everybody knew.

Once they were done, Boldo dismissed the servingmen.

"What's troubling you, Papa?" said Cristella. "Didn't you have a good day?"

Boldo could stand it no longer. "My poor darling!" he burst out. "I have done a terrible thing. I have put you, whom I love best in the world, in jeopardy!"

"In what?" said Cristella, who wasn't too good at the elder speech.

"In deadly danger!"

"How?"

"Can't tell you!" groaned the King.

"Nonsense!" snapped Dame Migraine. "Tell us at once!"

Boldo stammered out the story of his meeting with

Gulp the dragon, and of what was expected of Cristella the next evening.

"Of course she won't go. *I'll* go, with the Royal Guards — they would die for her, to a man. We shall sell our lives dearly! Meanwhile, you must both ride with an escort out of the kingdom, over the mountains, to the kingdom of my cousin Justin of Juniper, and stay till the dragon leaves. Baron Gnarl could go with you. Not a lady's man, exactly, but a heart of gold!"

Cristella ran and flung her arms around her father's neck. "Papa, I won't let you go!"

Dame Migraine, who had been stone-cold with horror, recovered her tongue. "Ah, Direful Day of Doom! Boldo's Bane and Blight!" Dame Migraine dropped into the elder speech when she wanted to be impressive.

"Aunt," Boldo said politely, "would you mind not talking that way? I've had enough of it."

"So, we leave," said the Dame. "And what if the dragon pursues us?"

"At least you will have had a start," said Boldo. "As for you, dear Aunt, have no fear. He *said* he had a delicate digestion."

Dame Migraine didn't know whether to be pleased with this or not, but, as was her rule, decided to take offense. She said she had always known something like this would come of the King's passion for the chase; it was most inconsiderate of him. Anybody else would have been satisfied with pheasants, but no, he had to burrow into a cave and find a dragon, who was only minding his own business, no doubt, and Boldo had been stupid and tactless, and this was the result. "Stop with Cristella? She'll only

26

make him hungrier! Don't slump Cristella!"

And he hadn't so far come up with an idea that would be of any use at all! "What can soldiers do against a dragon?" she sniffed, hiccuping now and then with fright and indignation. "Have we no sages who are versed in dragon lore?"

Grumble, seeing she wasn't feeding him any more, plunked his big head on her knee, rumbling indignantly at the King.

"Papa!" said Cristella. "What kind of beast *is* a dragon?"

"Reptile, I suppose," said Boldo, and he shuddered, seeing in his mind those claws and scales.

"Well," said Cristella, "this afternoon I went for a walk by myself, and I met a boy who can charm snakes . . ."

"The less said about that the better!" snapped Dame Migraine, who hadn't meant to let the King know her charge had escaped from under her very nose.

But Cristella went on and told him about Nip. When she came to the part about the gypsies, Dame Migraine sniffed until she sneezed.

"Such a funny boy!" Cristella said. "Do send for him, Papa! Really, he might think of something."

Boldo was ready by now to snatch at any straw — and at least sending for Nip would make for a delay. So word went forth, in the strictest secret, and when it had traveled down to the kitchen, a kitchen boy was found who knew who Nip was, and that he usually slept in the shed with his goats. They found him and woke him, and he was brought before the King, his hair full of straw, rubbing his eyes and yawning. Dame Migraine gave a sniff that outdid all her previous sniffs, and Grumble resniffed it even louder.

Nip nodded to the Princess, and then, prodded by the footman, went down on one knee to the King.

"You may stand," said the King. Nip rubbed his bare toes on the carpet; he had never felt anything so soft.

"Tell him, Papa!" cried Cristella.

Boldo told Nip the story. "So," he said, "my daughter thought, after you got her out of that scrape this afternoon — for which I am most grateful — you might be able to — to think of something, you know! She seems to think you have a — hum — influence over reptiles. Might have some idea about dealing with this, well, dragon."

Nip scratched his head. He had never yet heard of a dragon in Greengrim Forest, and he didn't believe in it. If there were such a beast anywhere in the kingdom, the animals would have told him. But something was afoot. Someone was up to tricks. He was not, however, going to tell the King so.

"A dragon!" he said. "Whew! Terrible beast!"

"Terrible, terrible!" agreed Boldo. "Smoke comes out of his snout like a — a giant teakettle. Could set the whole place afire, you know."

"Nip, the snakes like you," pleaded Cristella. "Maybe the dragon would. I never thought I'd be turned into a dragon's supper. But I don't want you to be either!" She tried to smile, because she was sure Nip would make a joke of danger.

"Hmm," said Nip. "I'll have to think."

"Yes, do!" said Boldo and Cristella.

The only sound was Dame Migraine drumming on the table with her bony fingers.

Finally Nip said, "Well, there might be something . . . it's worth trying."

"Take all my soldiers!" said Boldo.

"Not all. Half, maybe," said Dame Migraine. "The other half must come along to protect us. And help carry our baggage. I give you notice, Boldo, I am taking this silver flagon with me. It belonged to my mother, your grandmother, and was left to *me*."

Boldo sprang to his feet. "Flagons!" he roared. "Rags and tags and flagons! Do your haggling with the dragon!"

He hurled the flagon out of the window. It was the first time he had dared stand up to his aunt, and he could thank the dragon for it.

Dame Migraine sat with her mouth open.

"I don't want soldiers," said Nip. "They'd get in my way. What I want is all the pepper you can collect. A pail of it. The goats and I can do it, I think. We'll try."

"Pepper! for a dragon who breathes fire?" said Dame Migraine, recovering her speech.

Boldo's face fell. "That's so," he said. "No use, I'm afraid, boy. No use, you know."

"I've heard of fighting fire with fire," said Nip. "I'd like to try it."

He looked at the walls bristling with heads and antlers. "A dragon's head would look fine up there, over the fireplace," he said.

"Just the place!" said Boldo enthusiastically. "Of course," he added generously, "it would be *your* prize. And we should reward you, besides."

"Well, I'll be going," said Nip. He stopped at the door, and looked up at the heads again. "A reward, you said?"

"On my royal honor — whatever you ask," said Boldo.

"Within limits," said Dame Migraine quickly.

"What limits?" said Nip.

"None!" said Boldo, glaring at Dame Migraine.

"Well, it can wait. Till I come back."

"*If* you come back," said Dame Migraine hopefully. Cristella choked, and hid her face.

"I'll come back," said Nip. He still looked up at the heads. "Animals kill," he said, as though to himself. "But they kill for food, or to show who's chief. They don't

30

nail up their prey's heads, just for boasting."

No one said anything.

"You know," went on Nip, "that's what's hard to swallow about that dragon."

"What?" said Boldo.

"All that boasting," said Nip as he left.

"Whippersnapper!" said Dame Migraine. She rose and walked to the door. After a few steps, "Pepper!" and then, in a whisper, "Goats!"

Grumble stalked through the door after her, sneering over his shoulder.

5

Nᴇхт afternoon, the squadron for the defence of Princess Cristella marched out of the city of Barracoon, taking the road to Greengrim Forest. It consisted of twelve or fourteen of the biggest goats, led by Tuck, and followed by Nip, carrying a pail of pepper. Nip had decided his plan was worth trying, after conferring with some of the forest birds.

Birds were his chief source of information; they see a great deal of what is going on, and are great gossips. "A little bird told me" is often quite true, but most of us haven't understood what we were being told. Nip understood.

The city had been combed to find pepper, and in these days it was much harder to find — a rarity, brought from the East. Bewildered housewives wondered what was going on at the castle. The Chief Chef, Cherijello, they said, must be getting ready for a visiting Eastern potentate. Or was it to pack away furs? Or had Dame Migraine caught a chill, snooping around at night, and was the Chief Physician, Sir Gasper Gripe, preparing her a potion? The guardsmen could only say they didn't know, they had the King's orders. The housewives, shaking their heads, brought out their stores of pepper; so did the merchants and innkeepers, until a small pail had been collected.

Boldo and Cristella had come out to the goat pasture to see Nip off. Boldo had wanted to make something of a ceremony of it, with Royal Guardsmen standing at attention, but Nip had insisted on secrecy. And he meant to lead the goats on a roundabout way through the woods, not through the city.

Cristella's eyes were large and frightened, and she wanted to call the whole thing off, but Nip laughed and said he wouldn't miss it for anything.

"Don't go in the cave!" she said. "Be careful!"

Nip didn't answer; he grinned, and played a few toots on his pipe to call the goats to order. Before leaving, he brought up Tuck, the leader, and presented him to the King. Tuck took the honor calmly, as one royalty to another.

Boldo was not at all happy. "Well, boy!" he said — he couldn't bring himself to call him Nip, and he hadn't enjoyed what Nip had said about killing animals — "Fine thing you are doing! — poor fellow! — always remember you — put up a statue to you — but cheer up! you'll be back, of course — it'll be fine, fine!" At least Nip had no parents, he reflected, to whom his sad end would bring pain.

"I'll be back," said Nip. And he cut short the leave-taking and set off.

As they went through the woods, the goats chatted to pass the time. They fell to teasing one of their number, a lady goat named Burette, who, they said, was too fat to be sent out after the dragon.

One goat would say, "Did she get that way after she cleaned out the turnip field?"

33

Another, "No, it was after she ate the washing out to dry on the hedge."

A third, "I happen to know the truth. Burette found the moon fallen into the washing pool, and she drank it."

"She'll be floating up in the sky!"

"No, she's too fat for that. She'll stick in the trees, get caught in the branches."

"She can't be fatter than the moon, can she? Impossible!"

"Well, she's heavier. Maybe she'll get stuck on the church tower. They'll hear her bleating on Sunday, in church."

"They'll have to bring a ladder to get her down."

"No, they'll leave her till she's light enough to bounce back up in the sky. She'll go galloping across the sky at night, shining like the moon!"

"She'll go butting the stars around!"

It was decided that Burette was to be called the Horned Moon. "Poor dragon!" they said, "when the Horned Moon hits him!"

Goats spend a lot of time at this sort of poker-faced foolery. They call it "kidding."

Nip had kept them moving at a good pace, but of course it took them longer than it had the King on his horse, and it was close to six o'clock when they reached the quarry and the dragon's cave. All was quiet. The goats snorted at sight of the sheep bones.

"All right, I'm going in," said Nip. "Be ready, close to the cave. When I whistle, charge!"

He walked down the passageway. Gulp was there in the cave, a puff of smoke rising from each nostril.

"Ha!" he shouted. "Wouldst cozen me? Think I'd waste a crunch on your chicken bones? Not what I ordered at all! Take it away!"

Nip walked up to him and tossed the pail of pepper in the gaping snout. Then he moved to one side, whistling shrilly.

Strangling noises were coming from the dragon when the goats galloped in two by two. They crashed into the head, swerved to each side, to make way for the next two, and lined up along the wall. The last goats found they were butting two men, and no more dragon. Head and body had cracked, and crumbled into small pieces. Coughing and sneezing, the men inside crawled out from the wreckage, and stumbled toward the open air. The goats helped them on their way, butting them smartly. Outside the cave, they tripped and felled the men, and saw to it they stayed down.

"Who put you up to this?" said Nip.

The men looked sheepish, and one of them glanced up at the bushes over the cave's mouth. Lucky he did so, since Nip looked there too, and when he caught a stir and flash of metal he dodged just in time to avoid the arrow that whistled by his ear.

Knife in hand, Nip scrambled up into the bushes, the goats after him, but they saw only a horse and rider disappearing down a woodland path. The horse, they noted, had been tethered there while the rider crouched in hiding.

"Gnarl of Lumbago!" sang a little bird.

"The young one, it was," said the goats.

The two rascals were hobbling off through the bushes. Pepper and their buffeting by the goats had left no fight in them.

"We could catch them, easy enough," said Nip, "but I've an idea the King would just as soon not see them. Let them go! We know who sent them. Good butting, my valiant troops! On our way!"

6

Y ou can imagine the royal welcome that was waiting for Nip and the goats on their return. Since, at Nip's suggestion, nothing had been told the citizens of Barracoon, so they would not leave the city in a panic, it was a small welcoming party — merely the King and Cristella. Dame Migraine had refused to be present. She said she could not be expected to thank goats.

Riders had been sent to learn the fate of the small company, once it became clear that no fire-breathing dragon was going to descend on the city. They were surprised to find Nip and his goats walking homeward in the dark as though they'd been on a picnic.

Before they had left the cave, they had settled the matter of what they were going to tell the King.

Tuck, the oldest and wisest goat, said, "Why tell him? It would upset him very much, to know he was so stupid. He would lose the respect of all his people. If such a thing happened to me, I would no longer be leader. My goats would choose a younger, more sharp-sighted and sharp-witted goat to put in my place. I wouldn't wait for that; I would jump off a cliff. If these people had any sense, they wouldn't keep a king who has so little of it."

"What shall I tell him, then?" said Nip.

"Tell him the pepper drove the dragon blind and mad,

cast a spell on him, and he flew away. Say you don't think he will be back, but if he comes, you will take care of him."

So they buried the remains of the dragon, rolled stones in front of the cave, and left for Barracoon.

Nip knew that telling the King such a story could not be counted as the fair, open and honorable behavior which the monks had tried to teach him. He was deceiving him, playing a trick on him. But he saw it as a good trick, the kind goats like to play. Someone else, for sure, had been playing tricks on the King. He had an idea who that person was, but a less clear idea why it had been done. They had wanted to get hold of the Princess; they must have meant to use her in some way to their advantage. If he kept his mouth shut, he might find out more. The tricksters knew he had surprised their secret, but, if he kept it, they would think, "This is an ignorant oaf; he doesn't know who we are, or the power he holds over us. If he knew, he would try to make us pay." That was what they would have done in his place. But, if the King knew, *he* would *not* keep quiet about it. He would spill it all to the enemy — and then, would he take Nip's word against that of Gnarl, his chief baron?

Nip, in many ways, still thought as an animal would, and what Tuck said made sense to him. He was doing the King a kindness, he decided, in not letting him know his dragon had been a fake. Besides, he thought he saw a way to use the King's gratitude, backed by his promise, to make things better for his friends.

He would know them again, the men he had seen. If it crossed his mind that they would know *him* again, he brushed the matter aside. He could take care of himself. He laughed whenever he thought of them sneezing and choking over the pepper.

Boldo was, indeed, grateful. "Name your reward, my boy," he said, a bit uneasy because Dame Migraine had said Nip would surely ask for the Princess' hand, as they did in the stories. "Money? Jewels? A house of your own? The Order of the Dragon, which I shall create specially for you?"

"No, none of those things," said Nip, with a shudder at the word "house." "All I want is Your Majesty's promise — no more hunting in Croon. No more killing animals for sport."

Boldo was taken aback, but he had given his word. When he thought it over, it didn't look so bad. Somehow, since he had figured as the hunted, hunting had lost its zest for him. He was ready to call it off.

"I agree," he said. "In recognition of your noble deed, I hereby decree: no more hunting in Croon, none at all. What else can I do?"

"Well, you worked hard at killing animals, Your Majesty," said Nip. "You might try helping them, for a change."

"So I might," said Boldo, surprised.

"And we'd better keep this a secret," said Nip. "If the people knew about it — well, with Your Majesty's reputation as a great hunter, you can see how it would look. 'A mere boy overcome a dragon?' they'd say. 'Dragon feathers! Where's the dragon's head, Your Majesty? Where's his . . .'"

"Quite so, quite so," said Boldo hastily.

39

"Nip," said Princess Cristella, "you were brave. Was he very terrible?"

"Oh, just think of a lizard the size of a warhorse, spitting fire, buzzing like a hornet's nest!" said Nip.

"How dreadful! . . . I'd like you to have something to remember this by." She took a thin gold chain from

round her neck, with a gold charm strung on it, a galloping goat. "I'm sorry, it should be a dragon."

"Hey, that's the Horned Moon!" said Nip.

"What's that?"

"Oh, just a joke of the goats'. I mean about the goats. I do like it."

"Well, kneel then, silly," said Cristella, and she hung it around his neck. "And I've ordered a splendid meal sent to the goats," she said.

The King kept his word; there was no more hunting. The people were puzzled; at first they thought it was a joke, but those who disobeyed the decree were caught and punished, and they soon realized the King meant what he said. Hunting deer had always been the King's privilege, but they could no longer even snare a rabbit.

Boldo didn't stop at that. All the energy he had put into hunting animals, he now set to work at helping them. He went to council meetings so that he could introduce laws for the protection of animals, and he saw to it the laws were enforced.

He would now spend hours out in the forest, watching birds, watching all the animals. His hounds and falcons had to be trained *not* to hunt, which was a very hard job. The stags' and boars' heads on the walls were taken down. Hunters and falconers had to find other jobs that were more like work, which they disliked intensely. It was forbidden to kill rabbits, even rats and mice. As a result, gardens were invaded by rabbits, crops were ravaged by deer, and food stores by rats and mice. The people of Croon began to wonder if their king were losing his mind.

The ministers were concerned about it. Not only were the people complaining, but Croon was becoming a laughingstock to other nations. Formerly, animals had moved out of the country, and now some of the people were doing so. They wouldn't live under a crazy king, they said.

Boldo invited Nip to live at the castle, and so did Cristella, but he wouldn't come. He didn't want silk purses made out of his ears, he said. Cristella went to call on him, but the guards followed her, and after that he took his goats to graze far away.

Bits of the dragon story had leaked out, but no one believed it; they took it as one more sign that the king's wits were not what they had been.

In Castle Lumbago, sounds of a high baronial tantrum had been reported to the forest by an inquisitive owl.

"You let yourself be scared away by a boy and a few goats? Take that!"

"Ow, don't, Father! Those goats, you should 'a seen them — they weren't ordinary goats, no indeed! Demons, they were, coming for us! You'd 'a run too!"

"A likely story!"

Luckily for Cramp, the two other men bore out his story, and Gnarl, kicking them about the room, twisted his ankle and had to give it up. He had brought his son up to be a liar like himself, and now he didn't know what to believe. It even made him wonder if Boldo was such a fool as he looked. When Cramp suggested they have the goat boy hunted down and killed, Gnarl refused, thinking the boy must be only a tool. Better not alert whoever was his master until certain plans were ripe, rounded and perfect.

Dame Migraine was furious. She believed it had all been arranged by that imp Nip, to scare the King out of his hunts. She complained long and bitterly to her friend Baron Gnarl, winding up her woes as follows: "Baron, you will hardly believe this, but yesterday, in the casket where I keep my coronet, I found a *mouse!* with nasty

42

pink babies! and she bit my hand! And Cristella said, 'Yes, I put her there, it was such a good place, and you won't be needing your coronet for a few days, will you?' Creatures, creatures, everywhere! I tell you, Baron, something's got to be done!"

"I agree, dear lady! Mice, indeed! Snakes, next! We must save the kingdom from this madness. Yes, something's got to be done."

Grumble, behind them, rumbled his approval. The only animal he cared to see well treated was himself.

"At this rate," he growled, "I shall have no one to look down on! Everyone will be my equal! Why, I might as well have been born in the gutter, instead of with a pedigree going back to Globulus, who stood guard with Cerberus when Hades got too big for one dog to handle. Something's got to be done!"

7

O NE NIGHT, a year later, Nip, asleep in his shed, woke with a start, when a wolf crept in and nosed at him. Not that he was afraid of the wolf. It was Two-Bucks, a member of the wolf family he knew best out in the forest. The wolves came to see him at night now and then; he had made it clear they were not to touch his goats, and they had agreed. In return, he looked the other way when they picked up a sheep who had strayed out of bounds.

"Wake up, Nip!" said Two-Bucks, while Nip yawned and rubbed his eyes, thinking this was just a friendly visit. "They want to see you in the forest. Tuck knows; he will look after the goats. A small Council of Danger. Come, come. Hurry!"

"What danger?" said Nip, too sleepy to remember that in case of danger the animals never asked questions, but moved fast.

"You'll hear!" snapped Two-Bucks.

Nip was after him like his shadow. He could move as softly and see in the dark nearly as well as the wolf. He made sure his knife was at his belt; it was his claws.

A long way off in the forest, they came to a clearing with a great stone in the middle, and around it was a huddle of dark forms. Nip recognized his wolf friends, Lunger, Biter, Prowler, and the Chief of the Wolves, Crackabone, and beside them, not too close, the foxes. These he knew less well, as they are rather shy of the wolves, who look down on them, but he saw Dapper, their chief, was there, as was Burl, Chief of the Bears.

Nip knew there were several kinds of councils — Councils of Need, Grave Need, Danger, Close Danger. These councils could be small or large. They could include one or more of every kind of animal, or just a few kinds. They could include one or both of the Orders — that is, the Free and the Penned, as the tame animals were called by the forest. It was, of course, harder to get the Penned out for a council, since they would be shut up at night. A Grand High Council would include both orders, and was seldom held.

Nip knew that for even a small council of this sort, something serious must have happened. They were not held lightly.

He went up and stood before Crackabone, and said, "Here I am, Lord of the Wolves!"

"Sit, Nip," said Crackabone. "We sent Two-Bucks for you because you had to be told. You were in danger. Three of Gnarl's men were on their way to your shed — Dapper, here, saw them. They were sent to kill you."

"Hey! what an honor!" said Nip. "Why am I that important?"

"You interfered with his hunt before," said Crackabone. "Gnarl is taking no chances. He has a far bigger hunt on tonight; he is taking over the kingdom."

Nip sat up sharply. "Tell me!" he said.

"He has been planning this a long time. He is crafty, the old fox — um — snake! And he has many men, well

45

armed. Right now they will be surrounding the castle."

Nip leaped to his feet. "Come!" he said.

The wolves, foxes and bear didn't move. They blinked at him. "Why?" said Crackabone.

"If we get there first, we can warn the King!"

"You can't," said Crackabone. "They must be there now."

"Why wasn't I told? The birds must have known — you must have known!"

"We did," said Crackabone, carelessly. "What difference? They are all men. Except for you, who belong to us. We learned they were after you tonight, so we warned you. The others — let dog eat dog."

Nip leaped to his feet. "You'll see if it makes a difference! We had no more killing — I fixed that, didn't I? Now the killing will start again!"

Burl the Bear rose on his hind legs. "Bound to happen, Nip," he growled. "Men are men. Can't stop them killing for long."

"Maybe not," said Nip. "But I am a man too; I can't help what I am. These are my friends; I must help them."

"Why?"

Nip beat his hands together. "Because I should have told him! The King! I lied to him about the dragon — let him think it was real, and I drove it away! So he would stop killing. And now, what happens? Gnarl will kill him!"

Burl grinned. "He would have had him anyhow, sooner or later. A foolish man digs his own pit and falls in. You think the King would believe you? Not after honey-words from Gnarl—'He lies! My son drove off the dragon!' You changed nothing."

"Maybe — just maybe — he would have believed me! And then he would have taken steps against Gnarl. Anyhow, I should have given him the chance. It wasn't good, what I did. And what has come out of it, that's not good either. I must try to undo it."

"Too late now," said Crackabone. "It's only on your account the killing stopped. They are all eager to get back to it. Gnarl wants to kill you; without us, he would have. Would the others have gone on not killing us? No! It is you who upset the law and the balance. With you out of the way, all would have gone back to where it was."

"Maybe you are right, I don't know," said Nip wretchedly. "But I must do something."

"Just you alone? What can you do?"

"I don't know yet, but I'll try. That I swear! Maybe some of you'd help. Maybe not. My goats will."

There was a chilly silence. "What you must do," said Burl at last, "is stay away from that castle. Orders have gone out to kill you. You must move to the old wolves' cave and sleep there, where we can watch you."

A whirr of great wings, and a large bird landed on the lower branch of an oak tree. Two round yellow eyes gleamed at them.

"News! News!" said Blink the Owl. "Surprise Attack on the Castle! Gnarl and his Troops have Taken Over! Met with Almost No Resistance!" Blink always gave out his news like the town crier.

"You see?" said Crackabone. "It was easy."

"Greetings, Blink, and good landings! Tell us more.

47

What have they done with them? The King and the Princess?"

"King and Princess — Shut up in Dungeon Tower!" hooted Blink. "Treated with Care. Princess Cristella — Love Match Expected with Baron's Son, Cramp!"

Nip's knife had bitten deep into a tree, before he knew that he had moved.

"Now tell me I'm a fool!" he said, feeling sick and shaken.

"No. That we understand," said Crackabone. "Better than your words. But save it for Cramp."

"I'll save it — and double it," said Nip. "How do you know all this, Blink?"

"Usual grapevine," said Blink, stretching and flexing his wings to get all his feathers straight. "*You* know. Dogs tell, mice tell, birds tell. Dogs tell each other all they hear, but you can't trust them, sneaky things. On man's side, most of the time."

"Mmm," said Nip. "It makes sense. That's what they *would* do — why they wanted to get hold of her. Stupid of me not to see it."

He turned to the wolves, who hadn't moved. "All right, I'll stay here today, and think — think what's to be done. When it's dark, I'll be off to the city, and get some clothes somehow. Page's clothes, if I can. That way I can get into the castle. Only one who'd know me, most likely, is Cramp; the others had too much pepper in their eyes. Anyhow, it's a chance! Then I'll come back and think some more, till I've found a way. And when I've found it, we'll have a Grand High Council of Danger!"

The wolves grinned, tongues hanging out. "Listen to him! Why should we call that for you, Man?"

"For us all — I can show you!" said Nip. "The Two Orders, it must be. If the Penned will help, I think it can be done. Wolves, my brothers, give me this chance!"

They were silent, and Nip knew the whole thing hung in the balance.

"That will take time," said Crackabone at last, and Nip took a deep breath. "Two days at least. Count tomorrow, and then another tomorrow, at midnight."

"Thank you!" said Nip. "We stand together, we Beasts!"

8

AT THE CASTLE in Barracoon, everything had gone as Blink had reported.

Gnarl had been planning all year, in great secrecy, and this time nothing had interfered with his plans. The surprise was complete. Guards were disarmed and tied up before any resistance was possible. Gnarl's men moved into the castle and held it.

Boldo, asleep in bed, was wakened by a scuffle with his guards at the door. He would have leaped for his sword, but it was so long since he had even thought of it that he couldn't remember where he kept it.

"What does this mean?" he shouted.

"Baron Gnarl of Lumbago is taking over the kingdom," he was told. "Offer no resistance and you will be well treated. We are taking you into protective custody. Have no fear for your daughter; she will have the best of care."

Boldo put up all the resistance that an unarmed man in a nightshirt is capable of, but he was soon overpowered, and shut up in a room in the tower over the dungeons.

Cristella, it was true, had been treated with care. Two maids of honor whom she had never liked, because of their habit of whispering together in corners, woke her and told her that her father, for reasons of health, had been deposed, and that Baron Gnarl, by popular demand, was acting as regent, since she was not of age.

"It's not true! My father is perfectly healthy! Baron Gnarl has no right here! Nobody has demanded him! Send him away!"

But they were too many for her, and she was shut up in another tower room, with the two maids on guard.

Gnarl came to interview his prisoners in the morning. He told Boldo that he, Boldo, was a sick man, though he didn't know it, and it would be best for him to abdicate, but that all would come right in the end, and Princess Cristella's rights would be respected. A little confinement would be necessary, just at first, as a precautionary measure.

Boldo maintained a haughty silence while he spoke, but at the end he exploded. He refused to abdicate and demanded that he be instantly set at liberty, his daughter also, and that Gnarl and his men clear out.

Gnarl smiled, and said that Boldo would feel much better when he had had a good rest. Turning a deaf ear to Boldo's roars of rage, he left the room.

Gnarl then had an interview with Princess Cristella.

"Believe me, Your Highness, this is all for your own good! I happen to know, have known for some time, that the kingdom is in danger. Your dear father is not himself; he needs rest and care. All we want is to save your kingdom."

"Then let me go free — let my father go free!" Cristella was so angry that her voice did not even shake.

"Not just now, my dear, for your own sake! I shall

act as though I were your father — I *feel* as though I were your father!"

"I don't, at all!" said Cristella.

"Ah well, when you know me better . . . see, here is an order you may sign, so that I can carry on with everything just as you would like it. Pen, ink . . . Sign here, my dear, on the dotted line . . ."

Cristella picked up the inkwell and threw it at Gnarl. She had never done such a thing in her life, and it felt wonderful. The ink dribbled down his purple tunic.

"You'd better not do that again, my dear," said Gnarl with an ugly smile. "Upset, unbalanced, like your father. We'll have to bring in the doctor, and he might prescribe very little food for a while — *very* little! That would cool you off!"

Gnarl then requested the honor of an interview with Dame Migraine, who had snored through the night, and learned of the change of rule in the morning from her ladies-in-waiting. She sent a gracious reply, and greeted him with her most stately air.

"Honored Madam," said Gnarl, bowing low, "I regret exceedingly if we have inconvenienced you in any way. I trust I am acting only for the best interests of Croon, interests I know you too have very much at heart. If only your poor nephew had had them as you do!"

Dame Migraine said nothing, but curtsied deeply.

Gnarl came closer. "I shall be frank with you, dear lady. To many of us, it was clear that poor Boldo was very, very mixed up. All those animals! . . . I felt someone must act."

"Alas!" said Dame Migraine, raising her eyes. "Must I

confess? It has indeed entered my mind that my unfortunate nephew . . . mad, mad! Your Majesty has taken the only possible course of action."

Gnarl fairly purred. "Seeing eye to eye with you — nothing could make me happier! Your knowledge of the world — if only your nephew had a tenth of it, our little *coup d'état* would have been unnecessary. And now, may I count on the goodness of your heart, and your continuing in your exalted position as Dame in Charge of our little Princess?"

Dame Migraine curtsied again, even lower.

"She must not be deprived of her kingdom, and it seems to me there is a course open to us. You know my son, madam — a fine boy. Why not . . . ?"

"A most excellent solution, sire!"

"We do understand each other! Perhaps you might lay this matter before the Princess, in the most favorable light possible. So much depends on the presentation. She is not, naturally, too well disposed toward me at the moment. Surely, the sun never shone on a more perfect match!"

"And — her father's permission?" said Dame Migraine delicately.

"My dear lady! A madman's permission? Our one care with him will be to keep him from doing himself bodily harm. That tower window, you know — a long drop! And he could always starve himself."

"He could, of course," said Dame Migraine.

"A sad, sad case," said Gnarl.

"Direful, direful!" said Dame Migraine.

"Parlous!"

"Peradventurous!"

"Paregorical!"

This gave Gnarl the last word. Dame Migraine couldn't think of anything to beat it. So she sighed, simpered, and rolled her eyes. Gnarl bent low, and kissed a hand like an old chicken claw.

Meanwhile Rubeola was busy seeing that her wardrobe was stowed away in the Queen's cupboards — too small for it, she complained — and insisting that the ladies in waiting address her as "Your Majesty." She sent the Mistress of the Wardrobe to get Queen Florina's crown from the treasure vault, and tried it on. Cramp was in the long gallery, shooting arrows into the tapestry that showed Boldo the Ninth being crowned by large floating females representing Peace and Prosperity.

Evening had come, and Nip had made his way back through the forest to Barracoon. He crept up behind the shed where his goats were penned for the night, but he saw two shadows that didn't belong there crouching in one corner. Before he stole away, he hailed a passing mouse and asked him to give a message to the goats. Tuck he could count on. He hoped his friend would be able to come to the Council the following night, but it wouldn't be easy for him to slip away. If the new herd didn't know his goats too well, he might manage it.

Nip knew a place along the castle wall where a tree grew up close outside, so clear of lower branches that it was not thought dangerous. He had made use of it before, to steal cherries from a tree inside. Up it he slithered, and, hidden by its leafage, looked over the wall.

He was near the postern gate used by Cristella, and he saw this gate was no longer unguarded. Gnarl's men were all about, and they were a different breed from Boldo's; they looked tough and alert. They wore Gnarl's livery, clothing made in his colors, black and yellow, with his

arms, a salamander rampant, embroidered on the chest.

"The thing is to get into the castle," said Nip to himself. "With the key to the tower — and with the animals' help — I could sneak out the King and the Princess, get them away and across the border, to their cousin

King Juniper — he'd help them. Until then, I'd harass Gnarl and his crew, distract their attention. But first, I've got to find me a suit like that."

"Greetings, Nip!" He held his breath, then let it out. The voice came from the Snuffer, the chief castle watchdog, a large bloodhound. He was known to the castle as Trusty; the other animals called him the Snuffer, because of his excellent nose, which had just located Nip. He minded his own business, and was generally respected, even among the Free Animals.

"Greetings!" answered Nip. "How goes it, Snuffer?"

"What are you doing up there?" said the Snuffer, severely. "Not allowed. I ought to give the alarm. My duty, you know."

His face wrinkled up; he had acquired many wrinkles, puzzling over his duty.

"Duty to whom?" snorted Nip. "To Gnarl? I thought you worked for King Boldo."

"So I do, of course," sighed the Snuffer. "Now what should I do? All this is very confusing!"

"Well, it's King Boldo *I* want to help," said Nip. "And the Princess. Don't you want to help them? It's your duty, *I'd* say!"

"It is, it is," said the Snuffer. "At least, I *think* so. I'll have to think about it."

"Then be at the Council Clearing in Greengrim, to-morrow night at moonrise," said Nip.

Another shadow moved beside the Snuffer in the torch-light. "Ah, the Pouncer!" said Nip. This was the Chief Cat and Mouser, a privileged animal, who had the run of the kitchen. Other cats were allowed there only at his discretion. He was a tyrant, but fair, according to his own lights. Between him and the Snuffer, the two chiefs, there was an armed truce. The Pouncer was known in the kitchen as Tippet, a name he showed his contempt for by never answering to it. The Snuffer answered dutifully to Trusty.

"Pouncer, are you for a change of masters?" said Nip.

"Mrraow! Don't know yet. These are not good people. They will not be good to animals, or people either. But one master is much like another, as long as the cook remembers us. We don't depend on their favor like the dogs." He twitched his tail proudly, and the Snuffer growled deep in his throat.

"You'll soon see about that," said Nip. "Anyhow, come to the Council Clearing, will you, tomorrow night at moonrise? A Grand Council of High Danger."

"Oh, oh! Big words! Danger to us, you think?" yawned the Pouncer. "Why so?"

His shadow was gone; he had leaped up onto the wall. Behind the Snuffer, a large unwieldly shadow had appeared. Grumble was out taking the air, to help digest his dinner. The Pouncer, an old enemy, knew Grumble couldn't move fast enough to catch him, but he couldn't stand being near him. Dame Migraine used to perfume him because of his bad breath, and the other animals found the mixture simply awful. The Snuffer, though he thought perhaps it was his duty, was unable to like Grumble. He couldn't help seeing that Grumble never considered *his* duty, only his pleasure or his greed. He decided he would not give Nip away.

"Who are you talking to?" said Grumble.

"The Pouncer," said the Snuffer, thinking this was partly true.

"I smell somebody!" said Grumble, sniffing loudly.

"I smell nobody," said the Snuffer. "Just you."

"That's a story!" said Grumble. He raised his nose in the air and howled. At the same time, the Pouncer dropped onto his back, all claws out. Grumble's howl turned to yelps of pain.

Soldiers came running. "What's the matter with the dog?" one said. "He must have seen something."

"Cat jumped on your back, you'd howl too," said another.

Meanwhile Nip had slipped down from the tree and gone back to the forest.

9

Moonlight poured into the clearing in Greengrim Forest as though it were a cup hollowed out between the tall pines. The blackness under the pines was pricked by double points of light, gleaming on and off. More and more points appeared, and, as they moved into the clearing, they became the eyes in an animal's head. Arrowy shapes darted across the sky, and rustled in the branches. To a man, the silence would have been almost unbroken, but to the animals it was not a silence at all. It was like the tuning up of an orchestra.

Each kind of animal — fox, rabbit, deer, wolf — kept to its own group, and each group kept a little apart from the next one. Nip sat with Tuck, as silent as the animals, his arm around the goat's neck. He was glad Tuck had made it.

All movement died down; the animals sat quiet, alert and watchful. As though a signal had been given, a wolf leaped up on the flat stone in the middle, raised his head to the moon, and bayed, "I, Crackabone, Chief of the Wolves, proclaim a Grand High Council of Close Danger! It is the turn of the Deer to preside. Step forward, Deer!"

A giant stag, antlers spreading like branches, moved out of the shadows and took Crackabone's place on the stone.

"Pride, Chief of the Deer!" he belled. "Are we all here?"

A stirring, a rustling, coughs, growls and squeaks.

"Then step forward and name yourselves. First, the Penned Animals!"

Tuck walked out into the circle about the stone. "Tuck, Chief of the Goats! I stand for the goats and the other farm animals. They will agree to any action we decide on."

He fell back, and the Snuffer stalked into the clearing. "The Snuffer, Chief of the Dogs!" he bayed.

A large cat padded forward, spitting softly at the Snuffer as he passed him. "The Pouncer!" he yowled. "Chief of the Cats!"

"Is this all the Penned?" said Pride. "Then let us have the Free."

One chief took the place of another. After Crackabone, Burl and Dapper came Joggle the Hare, Flick the Squirrel, Weezer the Rat, Chillip the Mouse, Gloat the Frog, Shiver the Snake, Mudlip the Turtle. And others, too many to mention.

"The Birds?"

From a high branch came a scream — "Smite the Eagle, Chief of the Birds!" From a lower branch, a hoot, "Blink the Owl!" and, still lower, a piping — "Pirrowit the Wren, Chief of Small Birds!"

"Is this all?" said Pride.

An angry buzzing was heard. "And us? Always forgotten! We had a call and we are here! But no one thinks of us!"

"Pardon! Name yourselves," said Pride. It might have

been bodiless voices flying by that answered, "Whine the Fly . . . Pingg the Hornet . . . Wingle the Bee . . . Toggle the Ant . . . Wiff the Moth . . . Hipskip the Flea . . . Warp the Spider . . . Pistletwip the Mosquito!"

"Who else?" Nip stood up. "Nip, Member by Courtesy," he said.

"Good! we are here in number," Pride said, tossing his antlers. "I declare the Council open."

Flick the Squirrel, quivering with impatience, dashed back to the stone. "May I ask, why has a Council of Danger been called?"

Pride answered, "The Council has been called at the asking of our Member by Courtesy, Nip. It is for him to give his reasons."

Nip walked slowly to the stone, where he turned and faced the gathering.

"Members of the Council, you who have always given me your help, I am here to ask it again.

"First, let me ask you this. One land, two chiefs. To which will the kingdom belong?"

Crackabone said, "The question is foolish. To the stronger, because he can fight to keep it."

"What if we were stronger than he, and could drive him out? It would be good fun!"

"Why should we? The strong man is only following his own path!"

"What's to stop us crossing his path and turning it?"

Crackabone grinned. "Come to the point!" he said.

"Right! As you know by now, the King of this country has been seized, his place taken by another.

"The King, we all know, has not always been your friend. He has hunted and killed, and not for food — for sport."

A low growl of assent.

"But, after the trick played on him by Gnarl, the King changed his ways. He has forbidden hunting — made laws to protect you and your young. He has paid his debt as best he could.

"Now, Baron Gnarl, a far worse man, has risen against him. The King and his daughter are penned up.

"This is Close Danger to you all, as I see it. So I have called this council. Do you agree, and will you help?"

There was a long silence. Then Dapper the Fox minced his way to the rock, pluming his tail, sniffing this way and that. "Dead-eyes I may be, but I still don't see it. Close Danger? Useful Arrangements, maybe, but even that . . . Hm! Why? What is it to us if men are in danger?"

Nip said, "Does the forest fire care what it burns? Hard and cruel, this man is, and his son is worse. Killing will begin again."

Burl the Bear stood up, towering above them all except Pride. "If this is so, Nip, and we should help — how? What could we do? Your friends fear us worse than Gnarl. Would they let us near the castle? Hah! They'd shoot us down from the walls! Both sides would join against us."

"Open war, no," said Nip. "Tricks, tricks. Everyone doing his trick, and all the tricks falling together. Together, it could be done."

A deep rumbling from Burl: he was laughing. By the coughs and sniffs, the other animals were laughing too.

63

"Together?" said Burl. "Dogs and foxes? Cats and mice? Wolves and rabbits? Nip, the bee you swallowed in your honey has gone to your head!"

Chillip the Mouse ran up on the stone. "Mice, you said! I for one would like to help! Because of the Princess! She put my wife and her babies in with her aunt's coronet. Very kind of her, it was. But what could we do? Not all our enemies are Two-legs — they have four legs, they have wings!"

The animals snickered, and Chillip stamped defiantly, his whiskers quivering. "Who is *not* our enemy?" he shouted. "Can we come and go in the castle without Death stalking at our tails?" He hissed the last words at the Pouncer.

"When we have a Council," said Nip, "we have a truce, don't we? Couldn't we keep truce till the war is over?"

"We haven't Councils every night!" snarled the Pouncer. "Just how would we eat? We don't all live in castle kitchens!"

"A . . . a Food Storehouse," said Nip. "Armies always have that. You could all help there. Raids on barns and so on . . . And we'll need an Information Service. The Birds . . ."

"The Birds, did you say?" A broad shadow drifted to a lower branch.

"Yes, Smite. And let me ask the Birds this. You must have known what Gnarl was planning. Couldn't you have told me?"

"We knew! A camp of soldiers, his place has been. But we go there as little as possible. That son of his kills any

64

bird or beast that comes in sight. He mocked at your King's laws, and his people were afraid to tell. A pack of scurvy Two-legs!" He clicked his beak savagely, and said as an afterthought, "If we'd known he was after you, we would have told you."

"Now he is King, you will see what killing of birds and beasts can be!" said Nip.

Little Pirrowit flew up beside Smite. "They shot us before, they will shoot us again! What do we care if they shoot each other? It's that many less! Keep away from them, Nip! Stay in the forest!"

"I had hoped," said Nip, with a sick feeling inside, "that the Birds would lend me their powerful support."

Smite flapped his wings. "Your hope is vain. Put back your King on his throne, after all our people he has killed? His new laws — do they bring back to life?"

"If he were freed, his gratitude . . ."

"Man's gratitude! Warm yourself with hailstones!"

"I trust him," said Nip stubbornly.

Smite's voice was harsh, his eyes burned. "The more fool you! Our answer is no! Our help will *not* be given! Have we your permission, High Chief, to leave? This is our sleeping time."

"Go," said Pride. A flurry of wind appeared to rise and blow a lot of leaves out of the trees and away.

"No use, Nip!" growled Crackabone. "Forget it, and come back to us."

Nip set his teeth, and said, "If I have to do it alone, I will!"

Tuck snorted, and came to stand by his side. "I speak

for the Goats — we will help," he said. "The other Penned must speak for themselves. There has been no agreement."

The Snuffer followed him. "We are ready to help our masters," he said. "But so are the enemy's dogs . . . Ah, I see we have a friend from the castle!"

The dogs were pushing a large dog forward. Coyly, he waddled up to the stone, and stood as though waiting for applause.

"Is that a dog?" said Crackabone. "Looks more like pig to me. Yellow pig!" He sniffed at the new animal and drew back. "*Smells* like pig!" He said. The animal gave an outraged squeal.

"*Sounds* like pig!" said Dapper. The Snuffer put his paw protectively on the animal. "This," he said reprovingly, "is Sir Grumble, the Royal Pet!"

"Pet or pig, it smells funny," said Crackabone. "Who brought it?"

"Courtesy, courtesy, if you please! Is this how the Free receive guests? At our invitaton, Sir Grumble has come a long way to offer his help. Living where he does, he can be most useful. He will do all in his power to serve his masters. Isn't that so, Sir Grumble?"

Grumble snorted and wheezed. He had come because he was curious, rather than loyal to his masters. He considered himself bound only to his mistress, Dame Migraine, and he hadn't noticed her greatly put out by the change in rulers. He hadn't taken as much exercise in years, and he ached all over. And he had expected a far more grateful reception. The whole thing had been a mistake, and he wanted nothing more to do with these wild animals and this harebrained boy. But he didn't dare say so. Great grinning teeth, those wolves had!

"Do what I can," he snuffled. "Act as secret agent . . . inside castle. Hrrrmp!"

"Thank you," said Nip. "We shall be glad of your help." Grumble waddled out of sight.

A stir of surprise; the Pouncer had leaped onto the stone, head low, tail up. "We, the Cats, will help! I don't like that woman, the new Queen! She had me thrown out — Me!" His tail lashed.

A small figure bounced up and down beside him — Chillip the Mouse. "We'd help! If we could be safe from — you know who!"

"How about it, Pouncer?" said Nip.

At sight of Chillip, the Pouncer's whiskers twitched in spite of himself, but he controlled them, and licked his paws with care. "So long as we are not expected to be Cattibals," he said dryly.

"All that can be arranged," said Nip. "All right, a truce. Anybody else?"

Pride said, "It is the turn of the Free Animals to speak now. Can you give me one good reason, Nip, why we should join you?"

Nip shook his head sadly. "No, Pride. When you fight for others, is it for a reason? No! for a call in the blood. If you hear no call, it's no use."

"Isn't it for the Two-legs to rise against this man, if he is so bad? Not for us?"

"True. I hope they will, once they see what he's like. But they are like fat sheep, afraid. We can only show them the path."

Pride said, "Is there another animal who will join Nip?"

Silence. "I see," said Nip, feeling cold and tired. "That's all, then. Unless the Insects . . ." He meant this half jokingly.

Again the buzzing arose. "Sssso! You turn to us at last! The last to be thought of! Sssso!"

Nip's face had changed; he stood straighter. "Far from it, Pingg, Chief of the Hornets! I didn't think you'd be interested."

"Nor did you care! Our help is not wanted! Dead-eyes, all of you! What Four-legs can work with his brothers, plan, join for a purpose? None — only we! Look at the bees! Look at the ants!"

"Indeed," said Pride courteously, "we all know it — the Insect people do great things. They have a secret we have not."

"True, Pingg," said Nip. "For your size . . ."

"Size! Ssssize! Small as we are, we are millions! We were here on earth before any of you; we will be here when you are gone. We smell farther than you; we talk to each other far away! We fly faster than the birds! We build cities — we make wars!"

"In all wars, the flies grow fat," snarled Dapper.

Pingg was too excited to hear him, fortunately. "In a war, soldiers die! Our lives are short — we are not afraid to die. We are so many! But no — our help is not worth having!"

"No one said so," snapped Crackabone. "We bow, we bow!"

"You laugh! Good! We sssshow you! We attack

68

now — just as we would do against these men. You will ssssee! Ready?"

The clearing hummed angrily, dizzyingly, like an enormous hornet's nest. Helter-skelter, the animals bolted out of sight, under the trees. Nip, sweating, made himself sit still, but his arm shot up to hide his face.

"All right! Come back!" buzzed Pingg sweetly. "I was only joking!"

Sheepishly, the animals went back to their places. "Pingg, your point is proved," said Nip laughing. "Will you do me the honor of joining me?"

"Mmmmm. Perhaps we might join . . . Perhapssss."

"I am highly honored," said Nip. "And — also curious. May I ask why?"

"That will remain our ssssecret," said Pingg severely.

"Thank you, Pingg the Hornet," said Nip. "Your help will be beyond price."

"And now," said Pride, "it is late; the sun is about to rise. The Grand Council of High Danger is dismissed!"

10

THE FIRST shot, we might say, of the Nip and Tuck War
was fired the next morning.

Cristella was standing by her tower window, looking
out. There were no bars; who could get out of such a high
window? The room had been used by the Royal
Astronomer, and they had turned him out in such a hurry
that he had left some of his instruments behind. Cristella
had just peeked through the telescope, a small one that
had rolled into a corner, and had seen her father's statue,
the one on horseback in the public square. Workmen
were busy taking off the bronze head of Boldo and re-
placing it with one of Gnarl. Gnarl, a forethoughtful
man, knowing the head was removable, had ordered his
own head done by the Court Sculptor, Piff-Paffo, well in
advance of his seizing the power. Piff-Paffo had thought
it an odd but harmless notion, that the head was to be
made like that of the former Boldos. Now he had been
ordered to put the head on the statue, and to take the old
head home and melt it down.

Cristella was sad enough, looking out at the beautiful
world from which she was shut in, but it was better than
the walls of her room, with nothing more alive than spots
of flickering sunlight. What she saw through the telescope made her catch her breath; it looked so dreadfully
final. If Gnarl could take off a statue's head, would he

stop at a real one? She shivered, and hid her eyes.

The day was windy, with high bright clouds, and the swallows wheeled and darted in the sun. They appeared to be playing a game, riding a rumpeting gust of wind, diving back when it let them go. She wondered what their whispery cries meant; they sounded like part of the game, a flying-tag rhyme. If she could have understood it, the rhyme went something like this:

> *Swing high,*
> *Flicker by,*
> *Trick a gnat —*
> *Trick a fly!*
> *Low below,*
> *Walkers go,*
> *Creepers creep,*
> *Drowsy sheep*
> *Fall asleep —*
> *Swoop — sweep!*

The swallows had seen what was happening to the statue, and they were still laughing about it. Wild and giddy, drunk with the wind, they didn't see that someone below was very far from asleep. It was Cramp, Gnarl's son. He counted the moments lost when he wasn't shooting at something, and he had come out with his bow to pick off a few birds.

What with the wind and their own speed, the swallows were not in too much danger, but another bird had joined in the sport, a featherbrained young pigeon named Rocket. Rocket had always wished he were a swallow; he found pigeons dull and stodgy. He had been watching the game, and he couldn't resist joining in. Only, he couldn't fly as fast as the swallows, and one of Cramp's bolts nicked his wing. If it had been a fair hit, there would have been no more Rocket. As it was, he was stunned, nearly done for, but left with just enough strength to head for the nearest refuge. It happened to be Cristella's window.

He tumbled past Cristella and landed on the floor, wing bent, feathers awry. "Poor bird!" she said. "He's hurt — a broken wing, maybe. But he's alive."

She smoothed his feathers, straightened the wing as best she could, though Rocket fluttered wildly, and warmed him in her arms.

"Stay here with me, little pigeon — I'll care for you! I need a friend, and so do you."

Not long afterwards, she heard steps on the winding stone stairs outside. She hid Rocket in her bed, and sat on the bed. The guard outside was given an order, and the door unlocked.

It was Cramp himself. Cristella sat up as straight as she could, and looked through him.

Cramp bowed low, grinning. "Hey! Good day, Princess! Did you see my bird? Looked like I just hit one with an arrow, outside, and like he flew in here, but, sun being in my eyes, like, I couldn't be sure. You see him?"

Cristella made no answer.

"Aw, well," said Cramp, grinning more widely, "*I* don't care! You c'n have him, Princess! What's a bird? You're the only bird I want! Pretty little bird, all goldy feathers! You be nice to me and I'll see they let you out of your cage!"

Cristella began to understand the talk she had had with Dame Migraine, in which her great-aunt had dwelt on what a fine young man Cramp was, and how she had a duty to the kingdom. Her skin prickled.

"We'll be King and Queen some day, you know — that's how my father's planned it. What say? That's fine with me! We could have good times together. How 'bout it? What say?"

"I'd — I'd rather jump out of the window!" said Cristella.

"Aw now — give me a chance!" said Cramp. He sidled up to the bed and made as though to kiss her. Cristella slapped him.

Cramp swelled up with rage, and grabbed her wrists in his big hands. At that moment, a hornet flew in the window and stung him on the nose. He gave a yelp, and struck at the hornet. He managed to kill it, but others took its place, and he was stung all over the face. Howling, he turned and fled. The hornets buzzed in triumph, and flew back out the window.

Cristella gave a sigh. "You'd think they'd done it on purpose! How strange, how wonderful! Thank you, hornets, thank you!"

She turned to Rocket, and fed him a few crumbs.

The next blow struck didn't turn out so well.

That night, Nip had called his helpers, dogs, cats, goats, mice and insects, to a meeting on strategy, held in the pasture by the old sheepshed. The hornets had reported on their rout of Cramp, and the news was received with applause and congratulations. Nip was glad; he didn't like to think of Cramp and Cristella together. But he felt he should give a word of warning.

"In a war, we must work together. There has to be a plan. Before acting, we must meet here by night, and lay our plan."

"Sssso! We should have waited till we could report we had seen Cramp worrying the Princess?" said Pingg.

"Not at all—you were fine," said Nip hastily. "You did quite right. That was an emergency."

"What's that?" said Pingg.

"A pit in the path — a wolf in the underbrush — a housewife with a broom, when you are in her cabbage patch," said Tuck.

"Plans should leave room for emergencies," said Nip. "But if every soldier made a separate plan, it would be like every leg of the centipede running in a different direction. The man at the top has to see this doesn't happen — that's his job. He's the captain."

Wings whirred by, and something lit on the corner of the sheepshed.

"Greetings, Blink!" said Nip. "Are you here as one of the Birds, or just yourself?"

Blink received the question as though it were a new kind of mouse, snapping his beak and blinking his yellow eyes.

"Always on the Wing with the Latest News!" he hooted at last. "Tonight You — Are — It. Did I hear you speak of a Captain? Who? Who? You?"

"Don't call it an owl till it hatches, Blink," said Nip. "We're not there yet. That's for the army to decide. If they'd rather have one of themselves, it'll be fine with me. I'll work under him. What do you say, Beasts? Pick your captain."

There was an embarrassed silence. "Please," said the Snuffer at last, "just what does a captain do?"

"Why, he's your leader! You all know what a leader should do — why not each of you tell the others? Snuffer, you first. How should a captain lead?"

The Snuffer thought. "Find out what is his duty — what his master wants," he said, "and see this is done." The dogs growled their approval. Other animals, especially the cats, snarled, or spat.

"This time it might be hard to find out. Go on, Pouncer! What should a captain do?"

75

"He sharpens his claws — he stalks — he strikes fast, by night!"

"And his followers?"

"Oh, they do the same. Each for himself!"

"Purgo, Chief of the Pigs, what does a captain do?"

"Wear a gold sword and ride on a fine horse, with white feathers on his helmet! And — hrrmp! — get the best food."

"Chillip?"

"He hides, he spies out, he creeps into the enemy's corncrib, and he learns his plans."

Weezer said, "He bites!"

"Tuck?"

"The captain is wise and full of tricks. He watches his flock, and knows what each will do. He forgets no one. Bzz!"

"Pingg?" said Nip hastily.

"We don't worry about such things! Our captains are born to their job as our followers are born to theirs. No fusss!"

"All right, you have heard — pick your captain!"

Such a racket! The dogs said it must be the Snuffer — the cats, the Pouncer. Each animal wanted its own leader. Soon nothing could be heard but snapping, snarling, yowling and buzzing, and fur was beginning to fly.

As suddenly as it had begun, it stopped, and the animals shook themselves and looked at each other. The Snuffer limped over to Nip. "We think," he said, "you had better be Captain."

"No, no!" said Nip. "You'd never agree to follow a man."

"Better than following one of ourselves! Just for that. You belong to none of us, so you have no part in our quarrels. *And* you have a man's mind, so maybe you can outtrick these men."

The animals nudged Tuck. He said, "Nip, we will follow you, and do our best not to quarrel among ourselves — till this is over!"

"That's all I ask," said Nip. "Then you can throw me out, and eat each other up. And I want to say this — if I'm Captain, Tuck's my Counselor on Strategy! I'll do nothing without his advice and approval."

Tuck sneezed, to hide how pleased he was.

"Now, this is my plan, as far as it goes — not very far yet. We've got to get the King and the Princess out of the tower, and then out of the country. Once they are with King Justin, he'll help drive out Gnarl.

"So, first thing we must do is get hold of the tower keys. There must be another set, beside the ones the jailer carries."

"So there is!" squeaked Chillip the mouse. "In the guardroom. On the wall, there's a row of hooks. *This* side the row — " he waved his left paw at an imaginary wall — "and *so* many hooks from the end!" He bounced three times.

"Good work, Chillip! Third from the left. You and the cats must act as our spies inside the castle."

"Not the cats!" snarled the Pouncer. "They've been thrown out. Not a cat to be found in the castle. It seems we make Her Majesty, Queen Rrrrubeola, sneeze! Hhhah!"

"That's the kind of thing we need to know," said Nip.

77

"We can make use of it."

The dogs had begun to mutter in their throats. The Snuffer stepped forward. "May I remind you that *we* have not been thrown out? We, the house dogs, can come and go as we like. We could make a raid tonight, and bring you the keys."

"Since when can you come and go as you like by night?" said the Pouncer, with a sneer that curled back from his teeth. "By night you are all turned out except Grumble!"

"Grumble would help us! He'd open that loose window in the buttery," said the Snuffer. "Wouldn't you, Grumble?"

Grumble choked, and finally came out with, "Very risky, of course — see what I can do."

"Grumble, you barked at me in the tree," said Nip. "Are you sure what side you're on?"

"My mistake — didn't know you at first — help all I can — hmm, grmm."

Chillip bounced up and down. "Leave the keys to us! We're the only ones who can pass unnoticed!" He wiggled his nose proudly.

"How would you even lift the keys," snorted the Snuffer, "much less carry them? You think we dogs are stupid, or cowardly? Are we dogs, or are we mice?"

"I resent that!" said Chillip hotly. "An insult to the Free Mice, who obey no man. Snuffer, you'll eat those words! Are we mice, or are we dogs?" A chorus of growls and chitters.

"Stop it!" said Nip. "What did you promise me? A good idea, Snuffer, but I think it's too soon. Wait till I'm

78

inside the castle to let the prisoners out of the tower."

"No no!" barked the Snuffer. "Get the keys now — use when ready!"

"What do you say, Counselor?" said Nip.

"Let the Snuffer do it," said Tuck.

Nip started to object, but shut his mouth. He'd said he would ask Tuck's advice; he'd asked it. If he didn't take it, next time Tuck would keep his advice to himself.

"All right," he said unwillingly. "It needs planning, Snuffer. Let the mice be your scouts, and Grumble open the window. Take as few dogs as you can — two or three. Watch out for the guards — trick them, call them outside. Then you, Snuffer, stand up and get the keys off the hook."

"Yes, yes!" said the Snuffer, annoyed. "Exactly what I was planning."

"Third hook from the left, remember!" said Nip, thinking, "Let's hope Lord Chillip counted right!"

"Think it will be all right?" said Nip to Tuck, when the animals had left.

"All wrong," said Tuck, scratching his back with his horn.

"Then why . . . ?"

"Let him try! He'll learn not to be so cocky. They'll be willing to listen to you, next time."

"If I get too cocky," said Nip, "just butt me down!"

Tuck grinned, and chewed a daisy.

The guards in the guardroom were lolling about, some time after midnight, when a racket was heard down the corridor outside.

"What's going on there?" said the Captain of the Guards. "Sounds like all the dogs in Barracoon."

The dogs had not listened to Nip's advice. They all wanted to be in on the fun. Even some of the hunting pack from the kennels had jumped in through the buttery window when Grumble opened it. They were putting on an almighty rowdedow, yelping and yowling. All the guards came running to see what on earth was going on.

Once the coast was clear, the Snuffer stole into the guardroom, found the row of hooks, counted carefully, One, Two, Three, and stood up on his hind legs. He lifted the bunch of keys off the hook in his mouth, and turned to leave. Then something happened which he had not foreseen. Grumble had sneaked into the room after him; he now burst out yap-yammering and hobble-gobbling. No one would have dreamed he could make such a noise. The guards came running back, and caught the Snuffer with the keys in his mouth.

"Look at that, now!" said the Captain of the Guards. "Old Trusty pinching the keys! Who trained him to do that? What's he want with them?"

"Trusty's faithful to his old masters," said another guard. "Wants to let them loose."

"Old Grumble, he's faithful to us, at least," said another. "Knows what side his bread is buttered on."

"Well, someone put Trusty up to it," said the Captain. "Why would a dog want keys? Better chain him up."

The men drove the dogs out with kicks and blows,

and the Snuffer was beaten and chained up in the court-yard. He lay there sad and puzzled.

"Hi! *That*'s your masters for you!" said a small voice not far from his nose. Chillip had come to crow over him.

"Those were Gnarl's men, not my masters!" said the Snuffer.

"And who called them? Who gave you away?"

"You know who it was," said the Snuffer sadly. "An emergency. I did not foresee it. But how could I? A dog, let us in, and betray us? Be false to his masters?"

"Grumble has no master!" squeaked Chillip. "He has only a mistress — Dame Migraine! As false as he is! She is a traitor!"

"But then — he was doing his duty by her!" said the Snuffer, very much puzzled.

"Ah, but he was betraying the King, and betraying you."

"How mixed up it all is!" was all the Snuffer could say. "I shall have to think about it." He thought, and more wrinkles were added to those on his forehead.

"You'll have plenty of time for thinking," said Chillip meanly. He started off, and then came back.

"Don't think, it will hurt your head," he said. "I'll come and tell you stories about my children. I know quite a few of them. It'll help pass the time."

The Snuffer was thinking so hard he didn't hear just what Chillip had said, but he saw it was kindly meant, so he said, "Thank you, Chillip." Heavy with thought, his great head drooped lower and lower, and rested on his paws. Chillip sat down on one of his long ears, to keep off the night chill, and began a story about how his youngest, Willgrow, had seen himself in a piece of leg armor and had come home and said he had seen a monster. The Snuffer did not hear him. His face grew longer and longer, and a tear ran down and was lost in the wrinkles of his jaw.

11

"It just shows you," said Nip, the following night in
the pasture. "Where was our Service of Information?
Our spies? We should have known about Grumble." He
hadn't rubbed it in to the dogs; they were crestfallen
enough. The cats had not been so kind. They had said
nothing, but their whiskers smirked.

"*I* could have told you!" sniffed Chillip.

"Why didn't you, then?" Nip and the animals glared
at the mouse.

Chillip made himself as small as he could. "I meant
to," he squeaked. "But — those dogs! So nose-in-air!
'We, the Dogs — *we* can do it! Not you midges!' Ha!
Didn't we once free a lion?"

"Are the dogs your enemy now, or Gnarl?" said Nip.

"Well, I couldn't be *sure* Grumble would do what he
did. But everybody knows him for a puffed-up, per-
fumed pig!"

With an angry grunt, Purgo the pig rose and stumped
off down the hill.

"Oh, sorry!" said Chillip. "I meant to say, a puffed-up
bullfrog."

More grunts, and several smaller forms hopped away.

"Sorry, sorry!" said Chillip wildly. "What I *intended*
to say was a puffed-up popinjay!"

Everybody looked about uneasily, but no one moved. No popinjays. The pig and the frogs came back.

"Hey, you Beasts! There's a truce — remember?" said Nip.

"All I was going to say was, the dogs could have seen what Grumble was like as well as the mice," said Chillip. "Why didn't they?"

Weezer, a big frosty gray rat with fierce whiskers, came to his rescue. "Oh, the dogs — *they* stoop to see what's under their noses? Too far down!"

"Any more of those catty remarks . . ." growled one of the dogs.

The Pouncer snarled, Weezer squealed, and each animal showed his own signs — fur fluffing, teeth bared — of preparing for action.

"Stop it, all of you!" shouted Nip. "Smite's Screech! Do all captains have more trouble with their own followers than with the enemy?"

Tuck strolled out and tossed his head at the sheepshed roof, where the animals saw two yellow eyes, fixed and watchful.

"Aha! News of the Nights!" said Tuck. "Let's hear, Blink!"

"Animal Army Split in Combat! No Action against Enemy! More Fun Fighting with Friends!"

"You want that carried all over Croon?" said Tuck. "How Pingg will laugh!"

Blink gave a spine-chilling hoot, his way of laughing. The animals subsided guiltily.

"All right," said Nip. "Forget it, dogs and mice. The Birds say, Don't cry over a cracked egg — lay another!

Now, let's see. The hornets did well; how about the fleas? Hipskip, are you here?"

"Present!" said a voice we couldn't have heard, but Nip's ear had learned to catch it. It came from one dog's right ear.

"Lord of the Fleas, could you muster an army and move into the castle?"

"Hm. It will take a day or two. We move fast for our size, but we are small. I shall call my forces in from around the city. Word shall go out. Where do we aim the attack?"

"Every bed — every Two-legs in the castle! And — a special task force for Grumble. Leave the other dogs be. Now, Whine, Lord of the Flies?"

"He-e-e-ere!"

"Can you take over by day — invade the castle in force and harass the enemy?"

"We can — we can-n-n-n!"

"Good! Now, the Pouncer."

"Prrresent."

"You cats, you said, make the woman who calls herself Queen sneeze. Can we use that? Can you get into the castle?"

"Captain," said the Pouncer, and his eyes glowed green, "every morning she sits with her ladies in the Summer Pavilion. What if we arranged her a reception?"

"Right!" said Nip. "And listen, all of you. The sheepshed here is to be a storehouse for food, for whoever needs it. The cows and goats will drop in there when they have a chance; I have pails there — I'll milk them. Hens are sneaking off to lay eggs — dogs bringing bones.

And wait till you see the corn, oats, and so on the rats, mice, and squirrels have brought — carrots and turnips too! We must feed our Army!"

The animals, with one accord, made a dash for the sheepshed. Blink flew away, hooting:

Tu-wit, tu-woo,
   Tu-woo, tu-wit!
We bring to you
   The News that's Fit.

News of the Day,
   News of the Night —
News of the Dark,
   News of the Light.

Tonight, tu-woo,
   The News, you're It!
Tu-wit, tu-woo,
   Tu-woo, tu-wit!

Next morning being fine, Rubeola and her ladies-in-waiting went out to the Summer Pavilion. They settled there with their embroidery and tapestry, while one of them read aloud from an old romance.

Just as they were all crying happily over the story, Rubeola sneezed. Then she squealed. The ladies looked up, to find themselves in a circle of cats. The cats made no move or sound; they sat there, staring at Rubeola.

"Help! — atchoo — help!" yelled Rubeola. "Drive them away! I'm choking!"

The ladies flapped their arms, shooing the cats, but the cats ran here and there, and the ladies, with their long

skirts fell over them and each other. Rubeola went on
sneezing; her eyes streamed, she broke out in red welts.
The ladies screamed for help, until at last the guards came
and drove away the cats. Rubeola couldn't stop sneezing,
and they had to go back to the castle.

"That beats all!" said the guards to each other. "First
the dogs and now the cats! What's up?"

Two days later, the Snuffer woke after a good night's
sleep, though he was still chained, to find the castle in a
state of fuss and fidget. No one else had slept very much.
They were all heavy-eyed, and they were all scratching.

At first, without letting the others see them, but when they found that everyone was doing the same, they scratched openly, whispering together. The Snuffer was surprised; he couldn't remember a night when he had been so free of a desire to scratch. He spoke of it to some kennel dogs strolling by.

"Why, that's so!" they said. "Haven't had such a good night in ages!"

The maids did a good deal of scrubbing, sweeping, shaking out of beds and scattering of herbs and powders, but the next night was the same as the one before. Even Gnarl and Rubeola looked bleary-eyed, the Snuffer noticed, and very cross. And, to make matters worse, such a plague of flies had never been seen in the castle; they hovered in swarms, especially at meals. Moreover, moths had gotten into Rubeola's wardrobe, and left holes in her fine clothes. Enough, as Gnarl said, to drive you mad.

You may be wondering how the people of Croon felt about their new rulers. Were none of them ready to revolt? Were they all fickle, or chickenhearted? Not a loyal man among them?

To tell the truth, it had been "Comfortable Croon" for so long that its people had grown rather slow-witted. Slow wits make for slow moving. And Gnarl had done his work well, using what we would call a fifth column. His men had whispered it about, in taverns and public places, that Boldo had gone out of his mind — just look at him! First spending all his time at the hunt, then treating animals as though they were people — cracked, poor man! Next thing, he'd be hunting people — better lock him up, before that happens. Anyhow, it had never been he that ruled, not really: always Baron Gnarl and Dame Migraine. Might as well see things clear. Gnarl would be a fine, enlightened, progressive ruler — all the good things they had now, they would have double. As for little Cristella, the Princess — that was easy: she would marry Gnarl's son and be Queen.

People nodded their heads and said all this was so, just what they had been thinking. When Gnarl's men took over the castle, it was something of a jolt, but his men kept on talking. All would go on as before; Boldo and Cristella were getting the best of treatment. Gnarl made a speech in the public square. His life would be devoted to the well-being of Croon. His men clapped like anything. He had several splendid plans in mind, but to carry them out, it would be necessary — just for a time — to double the taxes. God Save Croon! God Save the King! The Royal Military Band struck up the Croon National Anthem.

The Royal Guard had at first declared they would remain faithful to Boldo, but, like Boldo, they had all been surprised in bed, and locked up before they knew where they were. Then Gnarl had talked to them, till they knew still less. They had never done much but parade, and, with good living, their uniforms had grown too tight. Gnarl had them fitted out with gorgeous black-and-yellow uniforms, and promised them a parade a week. Their duty, he said, was to stand by the Princess, who would be Queen, once she was married to

Cramp, and he himself had retired. They nodded wisely, and swore devotion to the Crown, not specifying who was to wear it.

Laws against hunting were repealed, and Cramp was in the forest from dawn to dark. He found the royal kennel most uncooperative, and swore a stupider lot of dogs had never been seen, so he used his own. The animals drew farther and farther back, up into the Gorge Rising.

The people began to learn there were many disagreeable things a king can do that Boldo had never done. Wherever they turned, they ran into special taxes, such as a tax to pay for the Royal Guards' uniforms. Whatever their trade, some official came around to pry into it, to order them to do things differently, and to pay a large share of the profits to the Crown. After work, they had been used to going to the taverns, for a sociable time; now, sly, cold-eyed men were everywhere, listening to all that was said, and, if anyone grumbled, he suddenly disappeared.

Even so, grumbling was there, deep down; you felt it in a tight mouth, a slow-burning look. Gnarl, following the principle of the Roman emperors, who kept their people happy with bread and circuses, announced that on the feast day of St. Vigoro, they would hold high festival. In the morning a tournament, which all might attend, and in the evening a Court of Love and Beauty.

A good festival is always welcome, and, looking forward to it, the people of Barracoon were happy and forgot their grumbling.

A day or two before the festival, one of Gnarl's pages

went for a walk in the forest. He came to a pool, so clear and cool-looking that he decided on a swim. He left his clothes on the bank, and plunged in. After splashing and dog-paddling, he came out, lay in the sun, and then went for his clothes. To his amazement, sitting on them was a large bear.

The page's teeth chattered, though not with cold. The bear looked calmly at him, and showed no signs of moving. The page backed off, and stood waiting. The bear sat on, scratching contentedly. Finally he got up, pawed over the clothes, and pushed aside a singlet, or long undershirt. He gave a snort that sounded like a laugh. Then he rolled up the clothes in a bundle, took them in his jaws, and ambled off into the forest.

The page had to go home in his singlet. His story of what had happened to his clothes was not believed at the castle, and he was dismissed.

12

THE SUN was high, and the stands about the lists, the field where the tournament was held, were full. For several days, Gnarl's heralds-at-arms had gone through the city, hanging the walls with tapestries and the windows with banners, the green banners of Croon and Gnarl's black-and-yellow. The lists were even gayer; pennons fluttered from tall poles, and shields with each knight's coat of arms were fastened along the overhanging roof of the main stand. All Barracoon was there; the upper crust occupied the stands, the middle class the space between stands and lists, and the common folk filled in the cracks and sat about on the higher ground above. In the main stand was the court, with Gnarl, Rubeola, Dame Migraine and the judges in the boxed-in part in the middle.

Cristella had been told she might attend, as though it were a great favor, and she trembled with joy to think of being outdoors again. "If I might go with my father," she said.

"No, too dangerous to let him out . . . Just think — you will be the Prince's lady, and wear his favor!"

"Then I won't go," she said, and she would not move, although they scowled blackly and told her she would be sorry.

Outside in their tents, the knights were arming.

Squires bustled about, helping their masters, and pages, like black and yellow lizards in their tights and jerkins, helping the squires — fastening a buckle here, tightening a strap there, or looking to the horses' gear. One page, a boy with black eyes and hair cut square, busied himself especially with the horses; as he went from one to the other, you would have thought he was talking to them. Monsters they had to be, to carry a knight in full armor, and the boy had to reach high to adjust the head armor about their ears. They twitched their ears at him, and tossed their heads.

Among the knights was Prince Cramp. No one knew exactly when he had been made a knight, and there was a good deal of fuss and etiquette about such things in those days, but Gnarl announced that Cramp had been given his accolade by King Frodo of Flare, whom nobody had ever heard of, and nobody dared object. Cramp's armor was the most splendid, and his horse, Bromide, the hugest. Unlucky were the pages that his squire collared and forced to help him; Cramp was in a temper, and ready with kicks and blows.

For the third time he had sent his squire to fetch a shield that suited him better, and he was alone. "Here, you, boy!" he shouted to the page busy with the horses.

"You called, my lord?" said the boy.

"Deaf, are you? Tighten this greave, bigmouth — fool of a squire's done it wrong. More, more!"

"The strap's twisted," said the boy. "I'll take it off and try again." He knelt with his back turned, working with the fastening. With his mailed foot, Cramp gave him a shove that sent him toppling. "Turn around, so's

93

I can see you're not fouling it up! Where'd you come from? — don't know your mug — or do I?"

"Yes, my lord," said the boy stolidly, picking himself up. "I was in the kitchen."

"That's why you've got clumsy greasy fingers — you'll have spots all over me! Hurry now!"

"There it is, my lord — just a minute, your left stirrup wants shortening . . ." The boy slipped to the other side of Bromide, so Cramp couldn't kick him again. Just then the squire reappeared, and by the time Cramp had cuffed him and scolded him, and looked around for the boy, the page had vanished.

"Ha! He'll keep," said Cramp grimly.

Patatataaaa! The trumpets sounded. The knights had mounted, and formed a procession. First came the trumpeters, holding high their long slender brass trumpets, and the tambourine-shakers. Then the heralds-at-arms, with their staffs, and poles with pennons like tongues of color licking the wind. The knights followed, dazzling in their armor; the crowd whooped, or clapped in a genteel way, according to its rank.

The proper ceremonies were observed — the heralds announcing each knight, each knight in turn naming Queen Rubeola as Queen of Love and Beauty for the tournament — they had been given such strong hints that they thought they'd better. Rubeola tried to hold her head high, like a queen, but she had no more neck than had Purgo the Pig's wife. Finally the knights retired, the judge rose and dropped his staff into the field, and the Herald Pursuivant, in a ringing voice, declared the tournament open.

94

This was to be a true tourney, and not a joust of one pair of knights after the other, so the knights came back in two groups, and lined up at each end of the field. Slowly they came closer, lances fixed and at the ready. The crowd held its breath. The knights spurred on their horses, who lumbered toward each other. Then, as though at a command, the lines broke. Each horse, to the stupefaction of the crowd, began kicking up its heels. "Bucking broncos at a rodeo!" we would have said. War-horses of those days were not really built for such capers, but they did their best. Hooves thundered, nostrils snorted, tails flew.

The knights were taken by surprise, and they had no experience riding bucking broncos. They were hampered by their armor, and also by their heavy lances, which tilted crazily, stuck in the ground, splintered, and helped to unhorse them. One after the other, the knights toppled to the ground with a deafening crash. For a while, mighty Bromide resisted this strange infection; he stood like a mountain. But suddenly his head flew down, his heels up, and he bounded about like a colt. Cramp flew over his head and landed bangety-whack; he didn't lie still, but rolled about and waved his arms.

The crowd, at first struck dumb, were now either hiding grins or laughing openly, according to how near they were sitting to Gnarl. Neither Gnarl nor Rubeola laughed at all; their faces were black. Gnarl called the Herald Pursuivant over, and spoke to him. The Herald Pursuivant then rode out and addressed the crowd.

"Oyez! Oyez!" he shouted, very much flustered. "Know ye that this Tournament, sith a strange indisposition hath seized upon the steeds, will be — er — post-poned until a later date. This afternoon will be held the Most Noble Court of Love and Beauty." He wheeled his

horse about — up went its heels, and the dignified herald went down in a heap.

The other horses, quiet at last, were led out of the

lists. There was a new look in their eyes, a waggish sparkle. "Haven't had so much fun since I was a colt!" it seemed to say.

Cramp's squire had reached him, and, alarmed by his tossing and groaning, had disarmed him on the spot. Other attendants had managed to catch and hold the now frantic Bromide. It was found that there were ants under the armor of both of them. None of the other horses revealed any ants when they were searched.

Cramp, his head in a daze from the toss he had taken, was led out of the lists. On his way, he stopped for a moment and looked at all the pages in sight. "Could that boy have done it? those ants?" he said to himself. "But how? and where'd I see him before?" He shook his head, and stumbled on.

That afternoon, a smaller and more select company gathered in front of the Summer Pavilion, where a dais had been erected, for Rubeola and the ladies of the court. They were a fine sight, in glowing velvets and brocades sprinkled with drops as though it had rained silver and gold over them. On each side of the dais were arranged allegorical figures, what we would call living statues. They represented Apollo with his lyre, Eros with his bow, and the Nine Muses.

A gong was struck, and a band of minstrels and troubadours filed out onto the greensward before the dais. They carried colics, quinseys and croups, and other musical instruments, to accompany their songs. Together they bowed low before the Queen, who blushed and simpered. One of them held up his hand and gave the pitch, and they burst into song.

> *Excellent Queen! Thy like who e'er did see?*
> *Citizens of Croon, come bow the knee!*
> *In reverence for one beyond compare —*
> *Royal Rubeola! Fairest of the fair!*

At that point, a strange voice joined the chorus — a donkey's bray. Other voices were added, until there was such a braying, whinnying, mooing, baaing, yowling, cackling, quacking, honking, squealing and grunting that no one could hear any more words. The noise was indescribable. The smirks came off the faces of the Court of Love and Beauty in a hurry, and were replaced by staring eyes and open mouths.

Gnarl, from his place, leaped up. "See what's going on out there!"

The audience turned red, trying to keep a straight face. The minstrels began again . . . "*Excellent Queen!*" . . . The noise redoubled. Pages and guards ran about, off scene and on, and the Master of Ceremonies came to tell His Majesty that a strange thing had happened — the farm animals, whom everyone had been too busy to pay much attention to, had somehow strayed out of their pens or their henyards — the dogs from their kennels — anyhow, they were milling about, and the minstrels' song had inspired them to join in. The farmhands had been sent for, and order would soon be restored.

"Someone must have let them out!" snarled Gnarl. "Find out who and skin him alive!"

At last all was quiet, or fairly, since moos and brays continued to be heard in the distance.

"Begin again!" shouted Gnarl, black as thunder.

The minstrels, their voices quavering, did so. *"Excellent Queen . . ."* and then it was they who were making strange noises, squawks and yelps. They slapped at their faces and legs as though they were doing some outlandish dance — in which they were joined by the ladies of the Court of Love and Beauty. The dumfounded audience soon saw what was the trouble — a dense cloud of mosquitoes and gnats had descended upon the scene — along with some flying ants, whose stings were like red-hot needles. Soon everyone, audience too, was slapping and dancing and crying aloud. The living statues, being the most lightly dressed, had the worst of it.

If anyone there had had very good eyes indeed, he would have seen Pistletwip, Lord of the Mosquitoes, in the thick of it, cheering on his men. He stung Gnarl neatly beneath the crown; Gnarl slapped at him, but only knocked his crown off. Pistletwip then stung Rubeola on the back of the neck. She leaped like a cow who has cropped a buttercup with a bee in it.

"Call it off!" gasped Gnarl. The Court of Love and Beauty picked up its skirts and fled for the castle.

As they fled, a large goat stalked onto the scene. It was Tuck. With his horn he forked up the golden laurel wreath, which Rubeola had let fall, and walked away with it over one eye.

"Anyone would say we were bewitched!" said Gnarl to Rubeola in their own room, as they rubbed healing ointment on their bites.

The audience ran home, slapping an occasional pursuer, but still laughing. They went on laughing all that evening and next day.

Cristella, in her tower, had seen the tournament through her telescope, and had laughed for the first time in many days. She was lonely and sad, and frightened, though she tried to be brave. Rocket's wing had long since healed, and he had flown back to his people, though he still came to see her. She hadn't been able to see what had happened to the Court of Love and Beauty until she saw them running to the castle. As she puzzled about it, Rocket landed on the window beside her.

"Hello, silly old bird! Back for crumbs, I suppose — what's that in your bill?"

Rocket dropped it in her hand, and she stared at it. "It's some child's toy — why, it's a goat! Made of twisted straw. A galloping goat! It's — why of course! It's the Horned Moon!"

She kissed Rocket's head, and her eyes shone. She felt wings, just like the day when she had run away from the castle. Somewhere, down there, was Nip, and he hadn't forgotten. He had sent her the Horned Moon.

13

THAT NIGHT, Nip was summoned to the clearing in Greengrim Forest, to a Small Council of Danger. A very small council; only Crackabone and Burl were there.

"This is an honor," said Nip rather coldly. He had not forgotten that they had turned down his appeal for help, although Burl had found him a page's suit. "May I ask why? . . ."

"Don't talk like a man," said Crackabone. "You know very well why. It's this war of yours — Nip's, Nip and Tuck's, War. You've done your best, you and the Penned and the Insects. But you haven't gotten very far yet. The King and the Princess are still in the tower. Well, we, the Free, have decided we will help you. That is, the Beasts of the Forest. I haven't spoken to the Birds, and, as far as I know, they haven't changed their minds. Smite is not one for changing his mind. Only in the molting season, if at all."

"That is . . . kind of you," said Nip, still wary. He saw there would be a condition.

"But . . ." said Crackabone.

"Ah . . ." said Nip.

"There will be a . . . bargain," said Crackabone. "You must promise to do something for us."

"So!" said Nip. "What is it?"

"Come back and live in the forest with us. Give up

being a man. You are not so happy with them, are you? You will be better off with us."

"Think of all you could teach us!" said Burl.

A deeper shadow fell over them. Pride, the stag, stood there. "Take your time, Nip," he said. "Take your time!"

"Why?" snapped Crackabone. "He has seen what they are like. Without us, they would have killed him as he slept."

"Perhaps," said Burl, in his honey-voice, "he will make peace between us and men."

Pride said, "No, never! Talk straight, Burl! Between us and man, there has never been anything but war. One man, one, we know for our friend, and that is you. We'll help for *your* sake — and perhaps in the hope — just hope — that some day there'll be other men like you!"

"The mad wolf bays for the moon!" snorted Crackabone.

"Maybe so," said Pride. "Just a crazy hope."

"Well," said Crackabone, "that is our bargain. Take it or leave it. Perhaps you don't need our help."

Nip said at last, slowly, "I agree. If you will all help me now, I will come back to the forest and live with you. Forever."

Without the full force, he didn't know if he could make it. He could harass the enemy, but could he turn them out? They were strongly entrenched. He needed all the help he could get.

And it was doubtful if he could wage a long war. He was in the castle now, but Cramp had come close to remembering his face. Once that happened . . . He must act fast.

"Swear it!" said Crackabone.

Nip took his knife, drew the point across his arm, and let the blood drip on the stone. "I swear," he said, "that I will come back to the forest, once the war is over!"

"Good!" said Crackabone. He came up and touched Nip with his nose; Burl rubbed his big snout against Nip's face. Then, since animals seldom waste words, they were gone into the night.

Pride said nothing. He stooped, and Nip felt the warm breath of his nostrils. Then he was gone.

Nip drew a long breath. He had won; they would help. But — what was it, that lump sticking in his throat? He stretched his arms, he jumped up and down, he hooted like Blink. He ought to be feeling like flying. But he didn't.

Until the tournament, Gnarl had gone on hoping he could persuade Cristella to marry Cramp, which would have made everything much easier for everybody. Dame Migraine had talked and talked to her about it.

"Firstly, it is your duty as the Princess to keep peace in the kingdom," she had told her. "Secondly, you will make things more comfortable that way for your father as well as yourself. Thirdly, Cramp is just the husband I would have chosen for you — a fine, upstanding young man — a bit wild now, but he only needs a wife to help him settle down . . . And . . ."

"Fourthly," said Cristella, "he is a poisonous little brute, and I shall never marry him!"

Boldo had been approached to use his influence with his daughter, but he had not cooperated.

"Marry my daughter to that little monster!" he had exploded. "I'd sooner see us both dead!"

"You will have that pleasure," said Gnarl, his face tangled into knots with rage. "At least, you would if you were alive and could see — "

After the tournament and the strange behavior of the animals, there had been a conference between Gnarl, Rubeola and Dame Migraine.

"Your Majesty," said Dame Migraine, rolling her eyes up, "I did my best!"

"No doubt, no doubt. The prisoners are out of their senses, I am afraid. If not worse."

"Obviously!" said Rubeola. "Rejecting my son! That snip!"

"Foul, fell and grisly portents, all!" said Gnarl in his deepest voice. "Smell you not powers of evil in the air?"

"Those cats!" said Rubeola with a shudder.

"The flies — and the other vermin, at night," said Gnarl. "Never, in our castle, have I seen such. Of course, my wife is an excellent housekeeper."

"The housekeeping in this castle has always been above reproach!" bleated Dame Migraine. "I saw to it personally. It is only since you have been here . . ."

"Madam, take care! You forget yourself! Did you ever keep house in a dungeon?"

"Your Majesty!" moaned Dame Migraine.

"Witchcraft, all this," said Rubeola, "working against us. The tournament! The horses! The other creatures!"

"*Somebody's* behind it!"

104

"The Princess always had a passion for animals," admitted Dame Migraine, "but — how could she make them do such things? It's not possible."

"You supervised her education, didn't you?" said Gnarl. "Are you sure she never learned any — um — incantations? Spells?"

"Never!" said Dame Migraine. "Would I have engaged any professors of *that* sort? They all had the best references. Not a sorcerer among them."

She saw she had said the wrong thing. "Of course, dear lady," said Rubeola, sweetly as a poisoned gumdrop, "but you weren't always present at the lessons, were you? Couldn't there have been someone who taught her a few spells on the sly? Perhaps your memory isn't as good as it was."

"Well . . . there was the Royal Astronomer," stammered Dame Migraine. "Such a quiet old man . . . It was careless of me — one should never trust those whose learning belongs to the night. He had a long beard and a tall cap, with the signs of the zodiac . . . of course, I know nothing of such matters."

"Where is he now?"

Dame Migraine didn't know. Guards were sent to find out. It was learned that the Royal Astronomer had left the country.

"Whoever's doing this is here!" said Gnarl.

"*Dear* Dame Migraine!" purred Rubeola. "You say you know *nothing* of witchcraft! Come now — when you were a girl, didn't you, just for fun, try a little — like everybody else? The way girls will — *I* remember! I say you can always recognize it, like dancing lessons

— it leaves a certain something, a charm, a distinction . . ."

"Well," said Dame Migraine, flattered, "I *did* attend a sort of class — just for fun, of course; it was all just fooling. And I never went beyond the third lesson. As a matter of fact, after the third lesson, old Mother Miasma was arrested and burned. Most unfortunate."

"Oh yes . . . that third lesson!" cooed Rubeola. "Changing yourself into an animal, wasn't it? So I was told!"

"No, it was putting a hump on your enemy's back," said Dame Migraine. "Mother Miasma picked the tax collector for demonstration purposes. He was furious, and had her denounced, tried and burned. But it was such fun at the time — we nearly died laughing!"

"How amusing!" said Rubeola. "You must show us some time!"

"Oh, I couldn't remember how it went to save my soul!" Dame Migraine giggled coyly.

"So you see, you can be a *great* help to us now, finding out who is doing this!" said Rubeola sweetly.

"Me? I told you — I've forgotten all I ever knew!"

"We've only your word for that!" snarled Gnarl. "You'd better find the guilty person — unless it's you!"

Dame Migraine turned an ugly yellow; she saw the trap she had fallen into.

"Your Majesty, my loyalty — my devotion! Perhaps I'd better tell you — the maids of honor who bring the Princess' meals have reported an odd thing. Several times they peeked through the loophole in her door, and they saw *mice* — dancing for her! A whole troop of them!

She was petting them and talking to them. And that bird she had, he comes, and she talks to him!"

At this, it was Rubeola's turn to change color. She really believed it all now. "What — what could she get hold of, up there, to work spells with?" she asked faintly.

"Oh, I daresay she could get hold of a few things!" sniffed Dame Migraine. "What with mice and birds and spiders . . . and then, Mother Miasma always told us, a really *good* sorceress doesn't need that stuff! It's all right there, in your own mind, she said. With the help, of course, of your — I mean *their* — evil master! . . . Oh, and the maids did see a kind of charm she was wearing, tied around her neck — a goat, made of straw."

"We must get rid of them right away!"

"All in good time, my dear," said Gnarl. "First, down to the dungeons with them. Then, a trial for witchcraft for Her Highness, and then . . ."

"Chop off her head?" said Rubeola hopefully.

"Witches are always burned, my dear. We must respect the traditions."

"That boy — the goatherd. You don't suppose he . . ."

"That gypsy vagabond? He's left the country by now. You mustn't worry, my dear; I'm right here to take care of everything, and I'm a very careful man. You're the Queen and I'm the King, and it's going to stay just that way!"

Cristella and Boldo were taken down to the dungeon that very evening. Alone, in their cells, they tried to be brave, but it was hard. The cells were black and damp and cold, with only straw to sleep on, and a tiny loophole

107

high up, whose light didn't even reach the floor.

Cristella was crying; it was the first time, but she was so lonely. She thought she was dreaming when a small warm creature slipped into her hand. Chillip had finally made his way in, with the help of a friendly mole who had dug a tunnel that connected with a crack in the floor. She

petted him and talked to him. He knew she wouldn't understand his stories, but he told her one anyhow.

It was the old story about the first mouse, a huge animal with antlers bigger than Pride's and longer legs, known as The Moose. When he galloped through the forest, snorting and bellowing, the animals ran away and hid. Even the terrible Cat of the time, with fierce long teeth, kept out of his way. He was King of the Forest. But he was too proud. He told the animals he was going out and kill Winter. So he caught Winter asleep, and he shut him up in a cave, and it was green for many moons.

So The Moose said, "Ha! Now Winter is dead, and I am going in to make myself a coat with his white fur, and dance on his bones!" So he went in, but Winter was not dead, only waiting. And Winter leaped out, and shut The Moose in the cave, and it was white and cold outside. And after many, many moons, Winter opened the cave and let out The Moose. But The Moose had shrunk and shrunk, down to the size he is now. And the animals looked at him and laughed, and said "Now you are the Mouse!"

"And ever since then," gabbled Chillip, "at the Winter Festival, we celebrate Moose Day. Willgrow and the other little mice tie twigs to each other's ears, for horns, and they do a dance. You'd like that — next time they do it, I'll . . ."

But Cristella was asleep.

14

THAT SAME night, a mouse named Week was hurrying up the path behind the castle toward the old sheepshed.

The sheepshed had become the meeting place for the animals, as well as a storehouse for provisions. Cows and goats strayed in to be milked; hens dropped in to lay their eggs. Forest animals were lending a hand now; squirrels brought nuts and corn, rabbits turned up with carrots and greens. Sometimes Nip was able to make off with odds and ends from the kitchen, cheese from the dairy, a rasher of bacon from the storehouse, but this was risky. It was no longer easy for him to get away, now that he was in Gnarl's service and wore his livery.

To keep away prying humans, Nip had taught the animals to behave as though the place were haunted. When a Two-legs came near, large spiders let themselves down over the doorway, and vipers stirred and hissed underfoot. Inside, rabbits drummed with hind paws and moaned pitifully. Usually the Two-legs decided he had business elsewhere; when a bold one tried to enter, the Lord of the Snakes, seven feet long, uncoiled himself in the doorway, and several bats flew squeaking in his face. He ran. By night, Blink the Owl hooted; cats let out unearthly screeches; a large bullfrog glunked in the corner; a trail of cheesecloth Nip had brought from the dairy waved in the doorway, and green eyes blinked from the darkness behind. The animals snickered when the Twolegs took to their heels.

Nip had arranged that some animal was always to be in charge at the sheepshed. Business was conducted on a barter basis; if you brought something eatable, you could take something in return. The animal in charge was sometimes Blink the Owl, sometimes the Pouncer, sometimes one of the dogs. Any arguments that might arise were to be settled not by personal or tribal combat, but by referring them to Blink. The sheepshed was to be called the Store, the animal in charge was the Storekeeper, and Blink was the Judge.

Week was a greedy mouse, and he was to pay dear for it. In his defense it must be said that life had not been easy for mice at the castle. Food was put away more carefully than it used to be. Rubeola had given orders. She had also decreed that all cats and mice were to be exterminated, and traps and poison were being put about. That day Week hadn't eaten much, and being a castle mouse he was too finicky to eat grass seed like a field mouse. He wanted cheese, and he was hoping very much that some would be waiting at the Store. "Even if I've brought no eatables," he said to himself, "I've brought news — surely they'll feed me for that! I've a hole inside as big as a cowbarn!"

It happened to be the Pouncer's night for keeping store, and the Pouncer too was hungry. He wasn't allowed in the castle any more; true, he had his own ways of getting in, but he knew about the poison and didn't dare eat any food left lying about. Nip, with Chillip's consent, had decreed that cats might eat field mice, as there were so many of them and they were not in active service, but might not touch the castle mice, who were now the only source of information on castle affairs.

No customers were in the Store at the time. Blink had not arrived to relieve him, and the Pouncer had important work ahead for that night. He thought he would just slip out and see if he could pick up a field mouse. "Hear that?" he said to himself. "That's the two sides of my stomach rubbing together and squeaking like a mouse. A few laps of milk — that's all I've had all day! Expect me to do a stalk like what's coming on *kitten food?*"

While he was outside, Week slipped in. No one there, and his eye fell on a fine round cheese. It was more than he could stand. One happy squeak, and his teeth were in it.

The Pouncer, disgruntled — no luck: the field mice were growing wary — came back, and there was Week. The Pouncer wasn't expecting castle mice up there, and he assumed this was a field mouse who had dropped in and was unlawfully making free with military supplies, which he, the Pouncer, was supposed to be protecting. He didn't stop to consider very long. He pounced, and swallowed up Week in three bites, tail and all.

"Trrrraitor!" he said. "Strrrictly forbidden! Myum, myum!" He washed his face, up to way back behind the ears.

Nip came in the door. "Hi, Pouncer!" he said. "All set? Have you got the plan straight? Last night it was right at your claw-tips!"

112

"My own part, yes — yours I couldn't swear to," said the Pouncer, yawning in his don't-waste-my-time rather than his sleepy yawn. "But it will come to me. What have you done so far?"

"So far, so good," said Nip. "I saw Hipskip, and he's told his people to lay off biting tonight in the castle. Last night they launched an all-out attack. It'll be the first night the Two-legs haven't been pestered for a long time, and they'll sleep sound. Dogs belonging to Gnarl's men won't be bitten either. And Pouncer! I put poppy juice in the dogs' food, so Gnarl's dogs wouldn't bother us. I squeezed and brewed it last night — I learned how from Brother Hubertus, when he had his toothaches. Not enough for the Two-legs — but I think it will be sleep tight all over the castle!"

The Pouncer licked his chops, still thinking of his dinner. "Oh, I forgot," said Nip, "here's a bite for you." He pulled out a bone with some meat on it.

"Verrry kind of you!" purred the Pouncer, "but why don't you eat it? You need it more than I do."

"I've eaten," said Nip. "What's the matter — are you sick?"

"No, no," said the Pouncer. "Just had a field mouse . . . If you really *can't*, we'll leave it . . . Well, just a bite . . ."

"Hurry up!" said Nip. "We've got to get over the wall now and in the buttery window; I left it unlatched. Then the keys . . ."

"First," said the Pouncer, his mouth full, "Grumble. Make sure where he is, asleep or not. I don't trust him. He gave the dogs away. This time he's not going to. Have you got your knife?"

"Sure I have. Grumble's your lookout. Don't let him see you and give the alarm."

"You think I would let him?" said the Pouncer, offended. "I was better than that as a kitten. I had lessons from the best tracker of his time — the Tail. We call it tailing, because of him."

"All *right!*" said Nip impatiently. "Come on! Our luck's not too good — there's a moon."

Two long muzzles nosed in at the door, each one with green eyes gleaming. "Friends — coming with us," said Nip. "Crackabone and Two-Bucks." The hair rose along the Pouncer's back, and the wolves growled.

"Friends!" Nip said. "Friends," said Crackabone, and the Pouncer relaxed. "But how will we get them in the castle?" he said.

"If my poppy juice works, it will be easy," said Nip. "Come on now, greedy old cat!"

The door in the wall used by the maids of honor was no longer unguarded; Gnarl's men were posted there, and the key was kept with the others in the guardroom. It had been too risky to steal it by daylight, but Nip had marked its place. He and the Pouncer climbed the wall by the tree, and crept along it till they reached a tower, by which it was not hard to reach the ground. Skirting the wall, they crept through the courts till they found the Snuffer, chained to his post.

"All clear?" whispered Nip.

"All clear," said the Snuffer. "Many sleeping, I think. Perhaps all. Soldiers bustling about, in the early evening, before supper. I don't know why."

As has been said, the castle was a ring of towers and buildings, connected by a wall, around open courts. Skirting this wall, they found the buttery window and slipped inside. In the kitchen, all was quiet indeed; what with the fleas' truce and the poppy juice, the castle slept well. Nobody in sight. "Wait here!" said Nip, and he made his way to the armory. Slipping through the guards, more than half of them asleep, the others nodding, he took the keys to the postern gate and to the tower, and was soon back in the kitchen. "I'm going to let in the wolves," he said. "They'll guard the gate, till we come with the King and the Princess. Up with you, now, and keep Grumble busy!"

The Pouncer, who had been investigating the larder, had a chicken wing in his mouth. "Eating *again?*" said Nip. The Pouncer put it down with dignity. "It so happens," he said, "that this is to lay a scent. I see garlic hanging on the wall. If you would be so kind as to stick a clove of it in this leg — Grumble is as fond of garlic as some cats of catnip." (The Pouncer liked catnip too, but no cat will admit this because he knows how silly he looks on a catnip miawl, as he calls it.)

"Beg your pardon," said Nip. "Well, I'm off to the tower. If I need your help I'll whistle — but keep Grumble away!"

The Pouncer went past the guards, who saw him no more than a shadow, and came to the large square tower with the royal apartments. He stole up the staircase. He knew that Grumble prowled at night, snooping into everyone's business, and that, since he never ate with the common dogs, he would have had no poppy juice. He intended, with the chicken leg, to keep him far from the dungeon tower.

A padding of heavy paws and click of toenails told him Grumble was already out on his rounds. Clumsy old cow! He had only to slip into the hall ahead, where Grumble couldn't fail to catch the scent.

Grumble's nose went up. What was this? Part cat, part chicken, and part — delicious! — garlic! Very likely the Pouncer himself, that hateful beast who had jumped on his back and prevented his calling attention to Nip on the wall — which would have stopped this whole silly business before it began. Since the night he had successfully called attention to the raiding party of dogs, he had been given the most unkind, horrid treatment by the other dogs, if he so much as showed his nose outside. Now, here was this insolent cat, flouting him! Raiding his larder! His nose went down, and slowly and heavily he followed the scent.

In bed, Dame Migraine sat up suddenly. She had remembered that fresh poisoned food, a new kind, had been put around for cats and mice. Would Grumble know enough not to eat it? Better that she go and call him back in the room.

Wrapping herself in a velvet robe, she went out into the hall. She could hear Grumble's toenails, click-click, and she went in that direction. By torchlight, she saw him ahead, sniffing along. Tracking down someone — an intruder? Such an intelligent dog — she had better follow and find out who he was on the trail of. She tiptoed after him.

116

Gnarl was not asleep either. The fleas' truce, far from putting him to sleep, made him more wakeful. He was puzzled. Could they really have been bewitched, and did this mean that the spell was over? Or was something else coming — something worse?

As you know — and as Nip would have known if the Pouncer had not eaten Chillip's messenger — Cristella and Boldo were no longer in the tower. That very night, Gnarl had had them moved down to the dungeons beneath. Cristella did not *look* like a witch, he said — but sorcery was afoot. Better be safe than sorry. And cooling her off down below might help her change her mind about Cramp; if not, well, they could stay there for good — as long as they lived, which needn't be too long.

He thought about the dungeon key. Why hadn't he kept it? The jailer would have one set; the other would be hanging in the armory. If she *could* cast spells — what was that he'd heard about the dog, Trusty, trying to steal the key? She might send another animal after it . . .

Should he send a serving man after it? What if *he* got bewitched? Better go himself.

Wearing a hooded jacket to hide his face, he minced along down the hall on his spider legs. Sodden fools, those lackeys! When he came back, he'd wake them up! From the gallery above the staircase, he caught sight of Dame Migraine, who had just reached the floor below, and was tiptoeing after Grumble.

This gave him a start. Like most bad men, he trusted nobody. Could Dame Migraine be the witch, after all?

She would fit the part better. Could she be plotting
against him? Had she bewitched the dog, who was tracking someone for her? And his guards, all asleep! He'd
give them something on the morrow. Meanwhile, he'd
follow.

Rubeola, who had insisted on sharing his room, so she
would always know where he was, woke up and found
she *didn't* know where he was. She too stepped out into
the hall, and down the gallery. She was in time to see him
creeping down the stairs, so intent he didn't hear her behind him. She stole after him.

None of them had seen the Pouncer, who was in his
element. An old castle was a wonderful place for a game
of hide-and-seek, and the Pouncer knew the castle like

the pads of his paws. He led them a chase. Up and down halls, corridors, lofty galleries, down to kitchens, bakehouses, pantries and butteries, dairies, storerooms, cellars and vaults. Unfortunately the garlic, which was luring Grumble, prevented the Pouncer from catching the scent of Dame Migraine, Gnarl and Rubeola, and he thought he was followed only by Grumble.

He slipped out onto the wall, and the others followed him in due course. The party wound along the battlements, among crenellations, machicolations, casemates, stalemates, turrets, gullets, follicles and ventricles, and vermiform appendixes. Sometimes they had to creep or climb or wriggle along. Dame Migraine and Rubeola

were out of breath and gasping, but none of them would give up.

Rounding a turret, the Pouncer thought he heard Nip's whistle. He wants me at the tower! he thought. If Grumble comes — well, we'll deal with him! Off we go!

When Nip had opened the tower door, he had found no guard, to his surprise. His knife had been ready, in case of trouble. Uneasy, he had run up the staircase — and had found the rooms empty; no prisoners. As he stood there stunned, Chillip scampered in. "Didn't you get my message?" he squeaked. "I sent a mouse to the Store — he hasn't come back! They've been moved, down to the dungeon below!"

"I got no message," said Nip. "The Pouncer was there — aha!" Some words of the Pouncer's had come back to him.

"Too bad, too bad," said Chillip. "All your trouble for nothing."

"Can you get into the dungeon?" said Nip.

"Not yet, but we're working on it," said Chillip. "We'll find holes."

"Good," said Nip. "Get in, and cheer up the Princess. I'll go back and try for the dungeon key." It struck him that if they could lock Grumble in the tower, he'd be out of the way. He was angry and wanted to lock up somebody. He ran to the guardroom, but there was no key. Passing by, Gnarl had pocketed it.

Back at the tower, Nip whistled, once, again, and the Pouncer appeared, swift and silent. "They've gone!" whispered Nip. "Up! Get Grumble in the room and I'll lock the door!"

Grumble, sniffing garlic, was not far behind. He broke
into his version of a run, and followed the Pouncer up the
stairs. Nip, hiding behind the door, saw to his amazement
Dame Migraine on the trail of Grumble. She started up
the stairs after him — then came Gnarl, then Rubeola.
Nip darted in after them, and up the stairs. The Pouncer
had deposited the drumstick in Cristella's room, under the
bed, and slipped out onto the stairs behind Grumble, who
pounced on the drumstick; he all but collided with Dame
Migraine, but in the dark she didn't see him, and he fled
down the stairs, avoiding Gnarl and Rubeola by jumping
into a loophole window. Nip was hard on their heels, and
he slammed and locked the door of the tower room after
them. He had the impression that Gnarl had grabbed
Dame Migraine, that she was screaming, Rubeola too, and
that there was a good deal of confusion inside.

Nip and the Pouncer turned to go, and found themselves face to face with Cramp.

He had joined the party at the end. It is probable that
he had been out late in town, and, coming back, had seen
the strange procession headed for the tower, and had decided to investigate. The moonlight fell on them. Cramp
caught Nip's arm. "Here!" he said. "What's going on
here? Who're you? . . . You're the goat-boy!"

Nip told the animals later, "I could have knifed him,
but I was afraid of what they'd do to the King and the
Princess!" So he only hit him hard enough to send him
sprawling, and ran for the postern gate, the Pouncer with
him. Cramp started yelling, and the prisoners in the tower

121

yelled too. Guards woke up, and ran toward the noise. "Catch that boy!" yelled Cramp. "Don't let him go!" Several guards ran along the wall to the gate, and the foremost blocked Nip and caught hold of him.

Two living missiles sprang out of the shadows, straight for the guards' throats. Crackabone and Two-Bucks had kept watch. The first guards went down flat; the others yelled in fright, and backed away. Nip and the cat were out of the gate in a flash, the wolves behind them; some of the guards drew their bows, but none with a good aim. Their hands were shaking.

"Ho!" said the Pouncer. "What a tail! The Tail himself never did better."

"Oh yes?" said Nip, furious. "Did you say you ate a field mouse before I got there, Pouncer?"

"Lucky, wasn't it?" said the Pouncer smugly. "Kept my strength up."

"Lucky! What you ate was Chillip's messenger! Coming to let us know they had been moved! If it hadn't been for you — if we'd gotten that message in time — we might have had them by now! So, due to your greediness, Cat . . ."

The Pouncer's whiskers twitched. "I never say I'm sorry," he snarled, but he looked guilty. "It *looked* like a field mouse. It went *down* like a field mouse. Why didn't it *tell* me?"

"Did you give it time?"

"Well. I *am* sorry. There! First time."

"Much good that does," said Nip bitterly. "They won't give us another chance at the castle. Cramp knows my face now. I'll have to stay away, and I can't wear these clothes. All your doing, Pouncer!"

"I *said* I was sorry," the Pouncer said, almost meekly. But, inside himself, he was saying, It *was* a good tail!

15

THE DAY after his unsuccessful attempt at the castle, Nip was in Barracoon, walking through the public square. He had been too troubled to sleep: he was up early, and had already clipped his hair and changed clothes with a chimney sweep he knew; he hoped he might get a job sweeping the castle chimneys, but he had learned from the town cats and dogs that they had just been swept. So it would be useless and dangerous to apply.

Funny, how it hurt to think of the little Princess down in that hole! How frightened she must be! No, she had good nerve; look how she had played up with the gypsies. She wouldn't let them break her down — somehow he knew that.

He was the one who felt down. If only he had known, last night! He might have had that key, and set her free. He must, he must find a better means of getting information. If only the Birds . . .

Blacked-up though he was, he must keep a wary eye out, and not be caught by Gnarl's men. No one was paying him any attention, at the moment. What ailed them? They were all looking over their shoulders and laughing, or doing their best to hide it. What at? Why, it was that statue on horseback — Boldo with Gnarl's head! Sure enough, something funny about it. All spotted and streaked, it looked. Scowling guards hurried up with pails of water and brushes, scrubbing at it. Passers-by nudged each other and hid their grins when the guards yelled at them to move on.

"Well, I never saw the like of that!" one man said to another. "Must have been a whole flock of them!"

Nip went closer, until a guard swore at him and told him to clear out.

He left, but his whole face had changed. A broad smile ran across it.

"The Birds!" he said, out loud. "The Birds are coming in!"

He broke into a run — you could almost call it a dance.

The Birds never explained just what decided them to enter the war. Birds, while good at information, aren't any good at explanations, and they never explain their own actions, as a group. They act, as they migrate, with a sudden swoop, as though the wind had picked them up. It may have been that they were moved by Cristella's caring for Rocket the pigeon. It is likely that they were not too sorry for her when she was shut up in the tower room. Men put birds in cages; if they choose to put princesses, that is their affair. But an underground dungeon is something different. No bird could live in an underground cage, and they didn't see how Cristella could. She would grieve her heart out, as they would. They wanted her let out.

That morning, Cristella was wakened in her cell by torches flaring, and men standing about her. They were in black, and wore masks. She was pulled to her feet. She felt for Chillip, but he was gone.

The men hustled her out the door, and along the corridor to a large underground room, where torches smoked along the walls. After her cell, the light dazzled her; it was several minutes before she saw her father, his hands chained together, and also Gnarl. She started toward her father, and he toward her, but the men held them apart.

"So here's our little Princess . . ." it was Gnarl's oily voice. "Greetings, greetings! We needed a friendly little chat. Entirely friendly, on our part. We only want to help you both."

"Then set us free!" said Boldo.

"Out of the question, unfortunately. You, my dear Boldo, are not master of yourself, and little Cristella has, so far, not been willing to arrange the whole matter for the best by marrying my son. And now, some very strange things have been going on — very strange — and we want to know why. So we have brought you here to ask you about it, in the friendliest way."

"So I see!" said Boldo, glancing about him. Cristella, following his eyes, saw there were odd-looking contraptions, heavy iron, along the wall — one like a bed, another, a wheel. She didn't know what they were, but her legs, for some reason, began to shake.

"Oh, this just happened to be a convenient room!" said Gnarl. "No intention at all of making use of those things — unless — but I am sure you are both reasonable people — at least, Cristella will have to be for both, since her father's wits are gone."

126

"Rot!" shouted Boldo, and lunged forward, but the guards held him fast.

"Now that is just the attitude you had better not take, old boy!" said Gnarl. "Not here, at any rate. We only want to ask Cristella what she knows about all this business — the dogs, the horses, the flies, all these crazy

animals! It's not natural, the way they've been acting. Someone's behind it — is it you?" he shot at her.

"I don't know what you're talking about. Behind what?" said Cristella.

"What's that?" Gnarl snatched at her straw goat, still hanging at her neck, and broke the cord.

"It's mine! Give it back!"

"Aha!" said Gnarl. "That's your charm, is it? We'll

just keep that, my little lady! And now, tell us who is helping you!"

"Nobody at all," said Cristella. "Who could help me?"

"Careful, now! See those things? They're to make stubborn people answer questions, by hurting them. We'd hate to hurt you, it would hurt us more than it would you, but we've got to know — the kingdom is in danger. So you'd better tell us all you know."

"I — I don't know what I'm supposed to tell you," said Cristella, and it came out as a gasp, because she was frightened.

"Well — we'll leave you fifteen minutes with your father, to talk it over! After that — you'd better talk!"

Gnarl and his men left the room. Cristella and her father drew very close.

"I'll see they take me instead!" said Boldo. "If that doesn't satisfy them, you'd better tell."

"Tell what? What do they want to know?"

"It's about the animals. Must have been doing something."

"Then it's Nip, behind it. And I'll never tell about him, never!"

The men were back again. "Your last chance — talk!" said Gnarl.

Cristella said nothing, but her teeth were chattering.

"Take me!" Boldo was struggling with his guards.

"Both in turn!" snarled Gnarl. "All right — the father first!"

The guards were leading him up to the iron cot when one of them stumbled and fell; he swore, and then screamed. A snake was twined about his leg, another about his neck. The floor was alive with them.

"Witches! Devils!" Screaming and striking at each other, the men fled from the room, Gnarl first; the bravest one slammed and locked the door.

What had happened was this: Chillip had overheard Gnarl and his men, had left by his tunnel and had alerted some birds, who had sped up to Nip in the sheepshed. At Nip's command, and with the birds and insects to spread the word, in no time a group of snakes had been gathered. The birds had formed an airlift, and had dropped the snakes inside the castle walls by the dungeon, where the mice had shown them the tunnel. They had wriggled through it to Cristella's cell, and down the corridor to the torture chamber, where they had entered with the men — a very neat tactical operation — unnoticed in the dark.

Cristella and Boldo, alone, looked at the floor writhing with snakes. Shiver, Lord of the Snakes, was there; he slithered up to Boldo, raised his head, and waited.

Boldo was almost as frightened as the guards and Gnarl, but, to his amazement, Cristella patted Shiver's head. "Thank you, thank you!" she said. "Papa, it *is* Nip! They're working for him! He's going to get us out, somehow!"

Boldo started to pat Shiver too, and then changed his mind. He bowed low, one king to another.

The moles, working in relays, made a branch tunnel that let the snakes out, that night. Many of them got beyond the walls by other tunnels, which the moles showed them, and Blink airlifted those who preferred it. They had never flown before, and were fascinated with it.

THE TRIAL of Cristella for sorcery was held the day after the scene in the torture chamber. The trembling guards had finally dared open the door, and had found the snakes gone. It was clear now that she was a witch, and that the goat boy was her companion. No doubt he had led her into the black arts, the day she had run off — she had signed a pact with him, learned the magic words.

Shuddery hints were let fall in Barracoon, about a princess who trafficked with cats and dogs, who bewitched horses from her tower, who commanded plagues of insects, who let wolves into the castle, snakes into the dungeon. The more simple-minded were appalled. The less simple-minded were beginning to suspect that Gnarl was a good brain-washer, as we would say, but they were in the minority. Witches were feared in those days, and few dared raise a voice in their favor, lest they be tarred with the same brush. What could *they* do, they said to themselves uneasily, remembering the little princess. Gnarl held the castle, and his men were well armed. And "Comfortable Croon" was so used to letting things slide.

So Cristella was brought up before the judges, and a form of examination was gone through.

"Did you, aided by a magical instrument, overlook the horses and lay them under a spell?"

"I had no magical instrument. It was the Royal Astronomer's telescope that he left behind. I could see them through that."

"You were directing them?"

"How could I? I was laughing at them."

"The dancing mice — you were talking to them?"

"I would have if I could, but I can't speak mouse language."

"You deny that you bewitched snakes, and drew them into the dungeon?"

"If I am supposed to tell the truth. But you don't seem to want me to."

She was sentenced to be taken out and burned the following day, unless she would confess, in which case it would be put off a day. They were so afraid of her that they didn't let her know her sentence, for fear she would find a more powerful spell yet.

On the next morning, the townspeople and countryfolk had crowded into the square before the cathedral, where a stake had been set up on one side, and a dais for the King, Queen and judges on the other. In between them was the statue of Boldo-Gnarl, covered with a large canvas to repel further attack by the birds, who had continued to favor it with their attentions.

Cristella was brought out in a cart; she was wearing a coarse gray shift, to make her look more like a witch, but it only made her look small and helpless, with her silver-gilt hair falling over it and her hands tied in front of her. There was murmuring in the crowd. The Public Prosecutor hurried over the list of her crimes . . .

"Whereas the witch Cristella did hold unlawful and accursed commerce with beasts, bending them to her will . . ."

Cristella looked about for her father, but it had been thought safer to leave him, and then see to it that he disappeared. As a further precaution, Dame Migraine, to her horrified surprise, had been locked in Cristella's dungeon cell, with Grumble.

Cristella knew by now that she was looked on as a witch, but she still hadn't taken it seriously — it was just a trick of Gnarl's. When she saw the stake and the faggots, her heart stopped, and then went on pounding: You are to die! You are to die!

"Whereas she did bewitch the horses at the Tournament of Love and Beauty, held by our most worshipful King, so that they did throw their masters . . ."

She looked about for Nip, but he was nowhere in sight. They had told her that he had been caught and killed — she hadn't believed them, but maybe it was so — if he were alive, he would have come.

"Witch Cristella, do you admit to dealings with the Devil your master?"

"No," said Cristella firmly. They would kill her anyhow. This was all she could do now, to show she was still a princess.

"Will you not admit it, that your soul may be saved?"

"No."

"Witch Cristella — you are condemned to be burned at the stake, and may God have mercy upon your soul!"

The executioner came forward to lead her to the stake.

The canvas over the King's statue bellied up, and fell

to the ground. The boy who had been astride behind the King leaped to his feet on the horse.

"People of Croon!" he shouted. "Your new master is sending an innocent girl to die a foul death! Look at her! Is she a witch? The tricks were all mine — mine and the beasts' — even your beasts fight for her! While you — Comfortable Croon! Crawling Croon! Will you see her burn before your eyes?"

"There's the wizard! Kill him!" shrieked Gnarl.

"No wizard, no spells!" shouted Nip. "Just a woods-boy who learned the beasts' talk! So they follow me! See now! Ready, Smite!"

"Shoot! Shoot!" yelled Gnarl to his archers. They fitted bolts to their crossbows.

Nip waved his arm, and, above the cathedral, the sky darkened. Clouds of birds flew in the archers' faces, beat at them with their wings, pecked at their eyes, and made it impossible for them to shoot. Down the one street that had been left open thundered a herd of goats, led by Tuck, and charged the soldiers. And all the dogs of the town were there, leaping at the throats of the soldiers, the guards, the executioner.

"Sorcery!" yelled Gnarl. "Shoot! Kill the beasts!"

The soldiers went for the animals with their swords. When the people saw their own dogs and goats being attacked, they shook themselves awake. They pulled out palings, they found stones, they ran into shops and armed themselves with what they found there, clubs and knives, axes, poles, butchers' cleavers, and with these they fell to.

Nip, from the statue, directed his army. He had chosen

133

his animals with care — none of the forest beasts, and no cats, since the Two-legs were too apt to connect them with witches. When the townsfolk joined in, he called off the Birds, who made it hard to see who was fighting who. Gnarl's soldiers, outnumbered and taken by surprise, put up only a halfhearted resistance. They had been terrified by the sudden madness of beasts and birds. Their master had cried "Sorcery!" and they had believed him.

Gnarl leaped down from the dais and caught up a crossbow, and aimed it at Nip. But a great bird swooped down and caught it out of his hands. "Thanks, Smite!" called Nip. Gnarl drew his dagger, and tried to climb up the statue. From far above, the crossbow came clattering down, struck him on the head, and knocked him flat.

Nip jumped down and ran to free Cristella. But she was gone.

Taking advantage of the confusion, Cramp had acted. He had jumped on a riderless horse, trampled through the crowd to Cristella's cart, caught her up on the saddle with him, her hands still tied, and ridden away. He was soon out of the city and into the forest, heading for Castle Lumbago.

He lashed his horse cruelly; the horse obeyed, but, once out in the forest, he left the forest road, and, for all Cramp could do, he kept on his way. They came to a clearing with a great flat stone, where the horse stopped, panting. Cramp cursed and beat him. At one end of the clearing he saw a line of wolves, drawn up, watching him.

Cramp was sweating with fright, but the horse seemed

unafraid. The wolves waited, their tongues lolling out. They came nearer.

Cramp did a most cowardly thing. He pushed Cristella off the saddle, so that she fell on the ground. Then he stood up and caught at a branch over his head, and climbed into the tree. It was a tall well-branched tree, and he climbed higher and higher.

"You won't have me!" he shouted. "Take the little witch!"

He went as high as he could, hoping to see the way to his castle. Then his head swam. Spots darted before his eyes, turning and twisting. He felt a stab of flame at his neck. Hornets — the terrible red hornets of the forest! He screamed and beat at them, yelling for help. He even called on Cristella to help him. But after three or four stings, he lost his hold. He fell, a long way, crashing through the branches, and landed asprawl, like a rag doll. He lay very still.

Cristella, her eyes shut, waited for the wolves. A cold nose sniffed at her, but nothing happened. She opened her eyes. Like dogs, one after another, the wolves trotted up and touched her with their noses. The last one gave her a poke, like a friendly dog who wants you to wake up and play with him. She smiled, but she didn't think her legs would hold her yet. The wolves trotted off into the forest.

To her amazement, the horse was still there, cropping grass. She thought her legs might work now, and pushed herself up, leaning on her bound hands. Once she looked over at the limp thing on the ground, and looked away quickly. She went up to the horse, very slowly at first,

136

but he showed no signs of running away. He let her push him over to the big stone; by climbing on that, she was able to get on his back.

She didn't know the way, but the horse did, and he set off at a walk, back the way they had come, to the road beyond the forest.

Far off, she saw a horseman, riding furiously, and she knew who it would be.

When Nip had missed her, he had seen that Cramp was missing too. A bird — Rocket — had lit on his shoulder, and had told him which way they had gone. He had found a horse and had followed. He pulled up beside her.

At first all they could do was to smile at each other, breathless. Then he took his knife and cut the ropes that tied her hands.

"Your father will be free by now," he said. "And — Cramp?"

Her eyes filled with tears and she couldn't speak, so he leaned over and kissed her.

"He fell out of the tree!" she said, shuddering. "The wolves — but they didn't touch him. He was afraid. So big, and such a bully! He climbed high up, and he fell. He was afraid."

"Fear can kill," he said.

"And so can a broken neck," sang a little bird in the hedge.

"Well, the war is over, little princess! Come — let's go!"

He grinned at her, and as they turned their horses, he looked back into the forest and laughed; then he whistled.

A file of gray wolves trotted out; behind them, a lumbering bear, and cubs. He spoke to them, and they fell into line behind the horses and trotted along the road.

As they went, the fields and the forest seemed to have come alive with beasts. They scuttered through the underbrush, or bounded over the grass; every hole or bush turned loose a furry creature. Pride appeared, with his mate and spotted fawns, and took his place after the horses. Snort the wild boar was there with his family; Dapper the fox, with a red-tailed tribe. They were followed by Joggle the hare, and rabbits of all sizes after him, long ears up and quivering. Then Flick the squirrel, with a noisy crew, and other small beasts.

The snakes and frogs stayed together in the rear; they didn't want to risk being stepped on by the Four-legged. Above, a flying column of bees, wasps, hornets and mosquitoes; fleas were offered a ride. Above the Insects were the Birds, swirling and swooping, high and low. Rocket the pigeon rode on Cristella's shoulder.

From the city and the surrounding fields came the Penned animals — horses, cows, goats and sheep, pigs, and barnyard fowls. They formed a sort of double file along the road with the Free Beasts, each treating the other with courtesy, and offering the right of way; in the end they trotted along side by side.

Along with the Penned animals came a troop of horsemen looking for Cristella; these turned and rode back to the city, to bring news of their coming. Word spread about Barracoon, and people rushed to the walls.

The Birds could be seen long before the others, but at last the townsfolk caught sight of the marching column.

All the bells in town were ringing, and Boldo had been set free and was waiting in the Square. He was rather dusty, but someone had brought his crown. The Snuffer, unchained, and the Pouncer were at his feet.

As the animals passed through the gate, the people cheered — such a noise had never been heard in all Croon. The animals trotted along, in quiet and orderly fashion, till they reached the Square — and then the Free Beasts turned about and went back to the forest.

17

A FEAST was held in the parks and gardens of the castle
to celebrate Boldo's return to the throne. Such a celebra-
tion had never before been seen. All Croon, all the animals, were invited, and they all came. Such music had
never been heard, because humans and animals had never
before made music together. Or such lights: beside
torches, colored lanterns and lights floating on the river,
fireflies wove swirls and wreaths between the trees. Or
such food! No meat was served, but, with mounds of
cheeses and platters of creamed eggs, buttered loaves and
honey, cakes and comfits and patties and fruits, no one
went hungry. Up in the sheepshed a feast was laid out for
the animals, and the Chief Chef, Cherijello, had spent even
more time and care over that one.

Nip was up at the sheepshed, seeing that all went well,
when one of the wolves told him, "Tomorrow night —
Council Clearing — moonrise!"

So his summons had come. He had been expecting it;
animals were prompt at keeping their word, he must be
the same. Now he would go back to the forest. Well! it
was what he had always wanted, wasn't it? No more
walls, no houses. No eating at table, no baths. No fuss,
no clothes. He was happy — yes, of course he was.

Next evening, in his herdsman's togs, he went to say

goodbye to the King. For good, it would be. The animals wouldn't want him to come back to the castle.

Boldo was very much upset, but said he quite understood, and wished he could do the same thing himself.

"Don't know what I'll do without you, my boy. I'll have to come out and consult you about things."

"Oh, you'll be all right now, Your Majesty," said Nip. "Well . . . goodbye . . ."

"Goodbye, dear boy. Oh — if you'd like to say goodbye to Cristella, she's in the garden, I think. Queen Florina's Alley."

Cristella was there in the garden. It was harder than he had expected, to explain why he had to go, and that it would be for good. Hard to tell her this was what he really wanted. Hard to talk at all, even, or to look at her.

"But why, Nip?"

"Because I promised. And because I'm more an animal, really — I don't belong here. It's where I should be."

"Nip — do you believe that?"

"Don't be silly! You can see it, can't you?"

"What I see," said Cristella, "is two legs, not four."

Nip said roughly, "You wouldn't understand what it feels like, being shut up in a castle."

"Wouldn't I?" said Cristella.

"I'm sorry," said Nip, and his voice cracked. "That was stupid. I forgot."

"My mind was never shut in," said Cristella. "But it will be now. Because you are going."

"I've got to go," said Nip.

141

"Won't you come back, sometimes?"

"Not often. They wouldn't like it."

"Then I'll come to see you. I'd stay, if you wanted."

"You couldn't," said Nip, his mouth stiff. "You will be Queen — Your Highness. Queens don't live in the forest." He looked at her very straight, so he would remember her like that, and then he bowed and left quickly. She would forget him, he thought. She would have to. And he too. Once out in the forest, he would forget.

"Nip," said Pride, "you know why you have been called?"

"I know," said Nip firmly. "I've come back. I gave my word. I'm ready."

"Ready to give up all that would be yours at court?" said Pride. "The honors waiting for you! The crown — the Princess!"

"You needn't bring all that up," said Nip. "I am going to be happy with you, and forget all about — everything else."

A silence. "No regrets?" said Pride at last. "Won't you be lonesome for men, and men's ways?"

"No!" said Nip. "I'll find things to do — I've got lots of ideas, right now — you'd be surprised. I wondered, could Tuck stay here with me?"

"No," said Pride. "Tuck must lead his flock. Each in his own place."

Winter had come and gone; the forest had grown warm and green and full of life. And a change had come over the Council Clearing. Three rough shelters had been put

142

up, facing the stone, beneath the trees. On the roofpole of one was a piece of slate with "Store" scratched on it; on the second, "Court," and the third, "School."

From under the one marked "Store," Nip and Two-Bucks the wolf came into the clearing. They were arguing.

"And another raid on the nuts!" said Nip. "You must keep track."

"Expect me to count those nuts every day?" snarled Two-Bucks. "I haven't got that many toes. And Flick's family helped collect them; why shouldn't they help themselves?"

"But that's not the idea, Two-Bucks! They should pay for them with some other food! And what happened to those three hens you brought in?"

"Haven't an idea," said Two-Bucks, licking his chops. "The foxes, they might know."

"You've got a feather stuck on your jowl," said Nip.

Two-Bucks wriggled. "Nip, I've been storekeeper long enough! It's someone else's turn."

"It's only been a week."

"Too long," said Two-Bucks. Something moved in the underbrush, and he was off like an arrow.

Nip sighed, and went into the Court. All he found was Blink, asleep on a stump.

"Wake up, lazy Owl!" Blink opened one eye, and shut it crossly.

"Nothing on hand this morning?" He tickled until Blink opened both eyes and croaked, "Only those squirrels again!"

"What about?"

143

"The usual — Swiffet's family, Flick's family — each says the other's stealing nuts from the store."

"Well, shut them up and try the case!"

"Try it! I've tried — I try no more! You say they must swear to tell the truth — I make them swear, and then what? Not a single one has told the truth so far — only what he *wants* to be the truth. You want me to sit here all morning listening to a lot of squirrels tell the truth? Even if it really was? Who cares?"

He flounced down off the stump. "I catch News on the wing!" he said. "I don't dig it out of the dungheap!" He was out of the door and away.

"Well!" said Nip. "Let's try the School!" Very quiet, there. He walked inside, and found only Burl, curled up asleep.

"Hey, Burl! Winter nap not over yet? And you were the one I counted on. Where's your school?"

Burl stretched, yawned, rolled over, rubbed his eyes. "Hmmm. Not so easy, Nip. Spring has come. Those cubs and young ones, they don't like being shut up. They want to prowl and howl and jowl, as they always do in spring. So . . ."

"So no one comes?"

"Well, this morning I was just a bit late myself," admitted Burl. "Just a scrap. I found some young willow leaves — first this year . . ."

Nip sat down. "Oh, it's no use! I thought I could teach you all something — but no one wants to learn!"

"Did *you*, when you were a cub?" said Burl.

"I've been a fool," said Nip. "We'll drop it."

The tinkle of a bell sounded in the clearing, and Nip

144

sprang up and out. "Tuck!"

The big goat allowed Nip to hug him and pull his beard. "How'd you get away? What's the basket of flowers for — are you Queen of the May?"

"For you," said Tuck. "From the Princess."

"Oh? . . . nice of her," said Nip.

Under the flowers Nip found a honey cake, with blue and silver sugar beads. "Here, Burl — Tuck, have a piece! Ummm, that's good!"

"All going well?" said Tuck.

"Not very," said Nip. "They don't like my games. They played them in the war: why not now?"

Tuck said, "Why don't you come back?"

"Are you getting as stupid as they are?" said Nip angrily. "I can't; you know that."

"Well, I'd better get back," said Tuck.

But they were no longer alone in the clearing; it was filling with animals. And Pride was there on the stone.

"What's going on?" said Nip.

"We've called a Council," said Pride. "Over you."

"Why blab about me?" said Nip rudely. "Worry about yourselves."

"So we have," said Pride. "Nip, it won't do."

"What won't?"

"Your plans," said Pride. "That Store, Court, School. There have been — complaints."

"What are they?" said Nip wearily.

"Let him hear," said Pride. The animals started shoving each other forward.

"Speak, Flick!"

"Please!" said Flick. "We don't like the *smell* of them.

145

Store smell, Court smell, School smell. Too *many* smells. It's not healthy."

"Is that all? I thought they would be fun. And — I had to do *something!*"

"Fun for you, but not for us! Nip, listen to me. You men have two powers — choice, and change. You can choose your way, and you can change it. Not we — no! Each of us was given his own way, and must follow it. When you try to make us change, to copy men — it's as if you had us walking on our hind legs!

"To us, you are the gods, Nip. Gods who hunt us down and destroy us. Maybe, some day, there will be kind gods, who help us. But that day is far ahead.

"So now, we follow our way — and you follow yours. The war did something for you that you didn't know about. It made you a man, at heart. You must go back to your own people. Each in his own place."

Nip's heart leaped in his chest, and he couldn't tell if it was more with pain or joy. Later on, Pride's words would come back to him, but now all he could think was: It's the first time they have said "You men" to me. Tuck pressed close against him.

"But I love you, my brothers!" he said, with a dry throat. "I want to help you."

"Knowing you," said Pride, "we know you will. But it must be in a way that leaves us free. And you too."

Burl said, "You can help us better living with men than you could out here. Because what comes to us lies in man's hands. He may, if he likes, drive us off the face of the earth."

At this, an angry buzzing arose. "Sssspeak for your-

146

ssself, Burl! If we had thought that, do you think we would have helped man?"

"I have always wondered," said Nip. "Why *did* you help?"

Pingg the Hornet hovered in front of him. "Becaussse! Some day we, the despised Insects, will take over the earth! It is so decreed! But first we must learn how man's mind works. How he does things. Ssso, we can learn to use your ways, and better than you. Sssssome day, we ssshall!"

"I see," said Nip. "So I was giving you lessons?"

"Yesss — yesss! A sssort of . . . sssort of . . ."

"Trial run?"

"You could call it that," said Pingg smugly.

"Just what," said Burl, "makes you Insects think you could do so much more than we Four-legged?"

"Because of what we have that you haven't."

"And that is?"

A long buzz. Both Nip and the Four-legged found the Insects' talk hard to follow, at times. It was a buzzing in the head, that gave you a headache if you listened too long.

"Org-an-izz-a-tion!" said Pingg. "Without that, you'll never win."

The animals twitched their skins lightly, as we would shrug our shoulders.

"We don't know what it is," said Burl, "but we don't want it. Too buzzy."

"Wait and see!" came a tiny voice. "When we flies are lords . . ."

Such a buzzing and zooming! "Flies, indeed! And we hornets!" "We bees!" "We mosquitoes!" A new war seemed about to break out.

Nip looked at Tuck, beside him. Tuck's beard was waggling. His head was back, and he was laughing. The other Four-legs were doing the same. They were squealing, and rolling on the ground.

Pride leaped into the buzzing swarm and tossed his antlers. "Stop! You sound like man!" he trumpeted. The buzzing quieted down.

Nip laughed and laughed, in great gusts, glad things had turned out this way, because he had felt like crying.

"Let's not start the War of the Future tonight!" he said. "All right, my Beasts, I will go back. But I will come often, and I hope you won't forget me. And — don't think of me *too* much as a man!"

18

BLINK the Owl was perched on the corner of the sheep-shed, in a grumpy frame of mind. After his talk with Nip, he had flown far to the border of Croon, to investigate a rumor that a hen there had laid a square egg. It proved to be false, and Blink was disgusted.

"At least it would have been News!" he muttered. "But where can you find News these days? Nip back in the forest — no good fights — that foolish Court — sheer waste, I call it! Back in the War, now — *that* was News! News every day! News every night! While now . . ."

He broke off. A couple of Two-legs — well, a Two-legs and a Skirt — had climbed the path without his noticing them, and had stopped by the shed. They were talking; they didn't notice him either. His eyes shone bright, and he leaned over to listen.

"You know, no matter how the stories end, you don't have to marry me, little princess. You mightn't like it at all. It would be different from what you're used to."

"It would! And one thing it wouldn't be is a one-two, one-two-three!"

"What's that?"

"You know — what you said. The day we met. It would be — what was it? — a sky-hopper!"

As the two shadows turned into one, there was a loud

"Tu-whoo!" and a joyful thuttering of wings. Blink was headed for Greengrim Forest.

So that was how it ended. Boldo made Nip his heir. Nip said he thought there had been enough Boldos, he would feel like a set of ninepins, and he preferred to be Salvo the First. And he refused to let his head be put on the statue; he said the Birds would find it too much of a joke to resist.

The Brothers who had raised Nip were asked again about the dark-skinned man who had left him at the monastery when he was a small boy. They had never seen the old man again, but they remembered he had treated the child with respect, as though he were of noble birth. Boldo had inquiries made in other lands; one of his messengers brought word of a far-off country where there had been a king killed by a wicked brother, and a baby spirited away by an old servant, never heard of again. Nip refused to go into the matter any further; he said Croon was enough of a kingdom for him, and he wanted no other.

A king must know many things he didn't, he found, if

he would keep his country in order, and Nip was determined to be a good king. He settled down to work hard. Boldo was delighted. He started to build a lodge out in the forest, where he meant to live as soon as Nip could take over the throne. He wanted to know the animals really well. He owed them his kingdom and his life, he said. Eventually he did live there, very quietly, with one attendant. The animals were shy of him at first, but gradually they got used to him, and even fond of him. The house was pretty messy, but he didn't mind. Sometimes Pride came to drink from the trough out in front. How proud he was when fox and wolf cubs were brought by their mothers to roll about his doorstep! And this he never knew, but it became the fashion among the Birds to have a hair from Boldo's beard in their nests.

As for the rest of Croon, Nip knew that both animals and people must go back to living by their own laws.

"We understand that you kill us for food," Pride said to him. "Many of us kill each other for food; some of us would kill you if we could. That is our law and yours. Only — leave us a place of our own!"

The people agreed they could not eat the animals who helped them be rid of Gnarl, and so new flocks of cows, goats, sheep and fowl had to be brought in from outside. Animals who had taken part in the war formed a sort of Animals' Legion, and lived until they died of old age. And Greengrim Forest was set aside as an animal sanctuary; there was to be no hunting, no killing of animals within its borders. How long this lasted we do not know. A king's promises are not always kept by his sons. But it lasted during the lifetime of Salvo the First, and even that of his children, who were brought up in friendship with the animals.

The people of Croon never forgot what it felt like to overthrow Gnarl's men, and of course they gave themselves credit for more than they really deserved. This worked out all right, because, after such a feat, they didn't want to go back to being "Comfortable Croonians," and felt it might be more fun to be "Come-along Croonians," and make their country stand for something more than comfort.

The war was also commemorated by a new coat of arms for Croon, with animals on it. A good deal of argument went on as to which ones should be used, since there wasn't room for them all. The animals were called on to help choose. After discussions that sounded rather like a new war, they finally settled on goats, wolves, birds and hornets, with a snake coiled into the crest — representing Penned, Free, Birds, Reptiles and Insects. Dogs and cats were appeased by figures of the Snuffer and the Pouncer set up on each side of St. Vigoro, over the cathedral door, and Chillip found himself between the saint's feet.

Grumble had to be chained up in the Snuffer's old place, otherwise every dog he met took it upon himself to give him a lesson. The Snuffer came by one day to make things clear to him . . . "Duty to your master, of course — all dogs will agree, but still, you are a dog, aren't you, not just a lady Two-legs' popsy-wopsy — there are other dogs, other masters — the world is bigger than you think, so is duty" . . . The Snuffer's eyes disappeared in a mass of wrinkles; he then dropped an old bone by Grumble. It had no more meat on it, but the Snuffer loved it. Grumble pretended to be grateful, but as soon as the Snuffer was out of sight he kicked it into the gutter.

Gnarl was never really himself after being hit on the head by the crossbow. He was taken to his castle and kept there under guard, but it was hardly necessary; he wandered in his wits. And an unfortunate thing happened to Rubeola. Just before Dame Migraine was released from her dungeon, she had worked herself into such a white-hot rage that she had remembered Mother Miasma's Third Lesson. So that, once the confusion of the final struggle had cleared away, Rubeola found herself with a hump on her back, and even a bit more. Dame Migraine had put such vigor into the spell that Rubeola not only had her hump, but a small drooping appendage over her nose. This, with the hump, made her look remarkably like a turkey-gobbler.

Boldo found it hard to decide what to do with Dame Migraine. She had shown herself no better than a traitor, hand in glove with his enemies. But she was his aunt, after all, and she wept and swore to be faithful. He didn't believe her, but he disliked the idea of locking her up, as he had been locked up.

Just then the Royal Painter-Sculptor, Piff-Paffo, had come to Boldo to ask if he shouldn't put the correct head back on the statue — it hadn't been destroyed, but hidden in a potato bin. Nip, who happened to be present — it was the day he left for the forest — suggested that two gargoyles be made, one of Dame Migraine, the other of Rubeola, and set up on the cathedral — not too high up: in plain sight from the ground. "By all means!" said Boldo, and so it was done. The two gargoyles looked so natural that the townsfolk went into fits of laughter whenever they passed them. When the two ladies appeared in public, there was a general snicker. This took the stiffening out of them both. Rubeola stayed in her castle and rarely appeared in public. Dame Migraine retired to a convent up in the mountains. She hoped to run the place, but the Abbess was a match for her, and set her many severe and ingenious penances. Dame Migraine thought longingly of Mother Miasma's Third Lesson, but she was afraid to apply it. St. Vigoro could hardly be held responsible for a hump on the Abbess.

Grumble went to the convent too, and the food there didn't suit him, nor his mistress either. He was seen begging along the highways, with a basket tied to his collar labeled "Please Feed the Poor Nuns!" When the Abbess learned of this, she was very angry, and both Grumble and Dame Migraine had to be content with barley soup for some time.

So now you can see how it was that the Four-legs, the Six-legs and the Wings fought the war on the side of — I was about to say, of Right and Justice, but those are big words, and it is doubtful whether the animals had ever heard of them. So let us say they were on the side of a few humans in distress. If they had their private reasons, well, so do most people when they go to war, but first there was the call in the blood.

It was, of course, a very small war, even for wars be-

154

fore nowadays when the world has become so small that there are no more small wars, because any war can bring us all in, buzzing like all the Insects together — so that it is really time we got around to running the world some other way, if we do not want to leave it all for the Insects.

And Nip? and Cristella? The reign of Salvo the First does not come within this story. We take leave of him as Nip. One scrap of information in a volume of Local Traditions and Superstitions of Croon may prove of interest. We are told that the old sheepshed above the castle kept its reputation of being haunted. In the days of Salvo the First, an apparition is said to have been seen there at night, by sober and reliable persons. A young fellow, a goatherd, sat at the door playing his pipes, and a beautiful maiden danced to them — silvery hair swirling like a comet's tail. All about her danced a flock of goats.

Also, among the annals of Barracoon is a copy of the announcement given by the town crier of the festivities held in honor of Boldo's return to the throne, which seem to have become an annual affair. Historians take it as a joke. We can take it as a farewell to Barracoon.

> Tomorrow night, in the castle gardens, will be held a High Feast and Celebration, in honor of King Boldo's return to his throne.
>
> Gates will open at 8 o'clock. Refreshments to the taste of all. In deference to our noble allies, *no flesh* will be served, but fruit, cakes, pies, sweets in abundance. Eggs by courtesy of the hens. Milk Bar by courtesy of the Cows. Wine Fountain by courtesy of King's Cellar.

Music by Tingalee the Troubadour and his Mad Minstrels. Also, for the first time, Chorus of Nightingales and Frogs.

Dancing — by Goats, Rabbits, Squirrels, Mice, Snakes, Moths and Small Animals. General Public is Invited to Join.

Clown Act by Burl Bear and Dapper Fox.

Wolf Howl at Moonrise.

Illuminations and Fireworks. Flicker of Fireflies. Glimmeration of Glowworms.

God Save the King! God Bless Our Beasts!